Unattached

by

Ildiko Szekely

To the most courageous woman I've ever known.

Prologue

1994
Budapest, Hungary

Nagyi doesn't seem to age. Her hair is short, a perfect fit for her dynamic personality. Today, it's darker brown with a hint of sunset. She lets my mom experiment with the coloring, so the shades of brown occasionally turn out fiery red.

"They're forcing me to go to court." The words rush out of my mouth, unfiltered. Nagyi lowers her crossword puzzle and gives me a pained, curious look.

She is the cornerstone of my life, the only person with whom I never have to pretend to be someone else. Nagyi. My grandmother.

"They're making me choose," I spit out the words, upset.

She listens to me patiently, without interruption, and bids me to continue with an encouraging smile.

"Dad wants to keep the alimony, because we are still living with him. Mom fights on principle, because at least one of us should go with her. And we all know that won't be Peter."

"Did she tell you that?" she asks gently.

I shake my head, near to tears. "I know she doesn't have a choice. I'm not stupid. The last few years have been… toxic.

The constant bickering, sleeping in different rooms, snide comments…" I sigh and look down at my hands, as if I'll find the answers there.

"I saw him hit her the other day. He isn't like that. He never touched her before, but… I saw it." I can't get a grip on the tumultuous storm that's gathering inside me. I swallow my tears and look at Nagyi pleadingly.

"I know I should go with her, but it's inconvenient." I bite my tongue as soon as I finish the sentence. My selfish words ring loudly in my ears. I wait for Nagyi to rebuke me, but she sits there without judgment. Her smile is tender and her eyes shine with compassion, which for some reason hurts even more. I feel the blood rising to my cheeks.

"Peter is no help," I continue, pressing on despite my burning face. "He finds ways to make my life a living hell, like it's his duty to make me feel miserable."

"Have you thought about how he might be feeling about all this?" Nagyi asks, her voice is soft and caring.

I shake my head unwittingly. "He is angry all the time," I counter defensively, "and takes his frustration out on me. He chases me with knives, throws books at me, and degrades me whenever he can." I think about Peter and search for the place in my heart where sibling love should be, but all I find is a gaping chasm.

"He called me a whore the other day," I begin, recalling the story more out of the need for absolution than to get him in trouble.

"I played along. I told him I just finished my shift with his girlfriend… He came up to me, slapped me across the face, and like a coward, ran into his room, barricading himself in there before I could retaliate. I was so angry, I punched through the window on his door." I pause to take a breath, absentmindedly tracing the line on the inside of my arm. Nagyi's eyes land on my scar, her eyes distant and sad.

"Dad just stood there, stunned. He didn't say a word. He grabbed my arm to make sure I didn't slice a vein. I don't think he knew what to say. I left the house bleeding," I continue, still playing with my scar.

"What scared me the most was the anger I felt." I admit it to her as much as to myself. "Not my bruised ego, or my bleeding arm."

I stop talking and look outside to avoid Nagyi's searching gaze. I watch the retreating city through the grimy window of our departing bus, which now emits a distinct odor from the trapped heat, gas fumes, and the sweating people crowded around us. My crossword puzzle lies untouched on my lap, too. Even the sunflower seeds, our staple snack on the ride to Felsogod, leave a bitter taste in my mouth this morning.

"I hate school," I say, still looking out the window. "I hate going to practice. I hate going home." I whine with all the self-righteous justification of a teenager.

"I feel guilty if I stay with Dad. I feel guilty if I stay with Mom. Dr. S. either ignores me or says he's had it with me. And there is Peter…" I let out a defeated sigh. I watch my breath fog up the window, blurring my view of the fading city.

"The other night, coming home from practice, this gypsy guy grabs my throat and waives a knife at me, demanding my new sneakers. I wasn't even scared. I was pissed. I kicked him in the groin and ran away."

I pull myself away from the window just to catch Nagyi's mouth twitch slightly. My lips curve, mimicking hers. I know I am being childish, fretting about everything, but she is the only one I can talk to without reservation, without feeling like I'm being judged. We sit for a while in silence as the bus makes its sluggish, jarring way out of the city, hacking up a smog storm in its wake.

I bite my lip in frustration. Nagyi puts her wrinkled, but still strong hand on mine and squeezes it gently.

"Remember when I was in the hospital?" she asks.

I vaguely remember it. Mom prevented me from going, just like she'd prevented me from going to Great-Grandma's funeral. By trying to protect me, she had inadvertently caused me more pain – I never had the chance to say a proper good-bye. I wonder if protecting us was also her reason for sticking around in an unhappy marriage for so long.

"You were still quite young," Nagyi says when I take too long to answer.

When she sees the blank look on my face, she continues. "I was diagnosed with stomach cancer," she says matter-of-factly, yet her grip on my hand is comforting.

"I went into surgery… it turned out to be a piece of shrapnel causing a little havoc," she says, rubbing her belly with a chuckle.

"Shrapnel?" I ask dubiously, finding my voice again.

"I have my scars, too," she says. "Souvenirs of the war."

She takes my hand and presses my finger to her forearm. There is a hardened lump under her skin.

"Is that… a shrapnel?" I ask stammering, looking at her, dumbstruck. She nods. "How?" I ask, still poking at her lump, fascinated.

"I was in the wrong place at the wrong time…" she says casually, her voice trailing off, "when a bomb exploded nearby."

"No way!" I exclaim with a mixture of awe and horror and utter respect.

She nods and gives me an affectionate smile as if she just told me what she had for breakfast. Her smile is genuine – the kind that makes you want to divulge your deepest, darkest secrets.

"Last year your mom dragged me to a dermatologist, because I started getting hives," she says, waiving her hand over her body, like the bomb wasn't even the punchline. I wait for it with fervent anticipation.

"It was my liver…" she says, pausing to take a deep breath. "It was in really bad shape."

"Why?" I ask, aghast.

"I was given Hepatitis C blood during the surgery."

I am confused. "The doctors gave you bad blood?"

She nods without any hint of being upset. "You could say that."

"Is that serious?" I ask, still stunned and perplexed.

"It's an infection that can destroy your liver."

She sees the shock on my face and squeezes my hand with reassurance. My petty complaints grow even more insignificant in light of her story. I am amazed at her composure, with the delicate formality with which she delivers her tragedy. She must see the fear in my eyes.

"There is no need for worry," she says encouragingly. "I am well, now."

I brave a smile.

"There are people who believe our lives are nothing but a sequence of coincidences. Your mom calls it fate. Whether it is coincidence or fate, I believe that we are only burdened with as much as we can endure. My series of events led me here, sitting with you, and I wouldn't change that for the world," she says, and offers me more sunflower seeds.

I have so many questions for her, as she rarely, if ever, talks about her life. But something tells me it's not the right time. I grab a seed with my thumb and forefinger, crack it open with my front teeth, and pull the heart out with my tongue – the way she'd taught me. It no longer tastes bitter.

"I don't believe in regrets," she says, and offers me a cup to deposit the shells. "Good judgment is based on experience, but experience is born from bad judgment. That is life, Ollie."

I watch her with admiration, waiting eagerly for her to finish her thought. She nudges me to take another seed.

"I can tell there is a lot going on inside of you and you are looking for guidance. But the truest guide is your heart." She takes my hand once again and plants a kiss on it.

"Life is unpredictable, Ollie, but it is defined by the choices we make. Happiness doesn't grow on trees. It's not a grand design. It is a choice. You can choose to mope around and lick your wounds," she says with a chuckle, "or choose to find happiness in the everyday moments life has to offer, like swimming, or coming with me to Felsogod," she says and takes a deep breath.

"Tragedy is part of life, but happiness – *true* happiness – that's a conscious decision, and it's built on shared moments of fulfillment – of love." She grabs a sunflower seed and pops it into her mouth with a satisfied grin. I can't help but grin back at her foolishly.

"You have one life, Ollie. Make it yours. Dream big and pursue your dreams with that relentless passion I know you possess. Life goes by too fast to idle around and wait for others to make your decisions for you."

Chapter 1

1982
Budapest, Hungary

Smog covers the city in a fog-like haze. It's hot and muggy and smells like burning asphalt. I cover my nose with my hand to block the stench; it scratches my throat.

Mother is dragging me along the crowded street. I'm desperately trying to keep up. People are coming and going, walking by us (nearly colliding) without a second glance. Their shirts are stained with sweat. Their faces are grim.

Mother is in a hurry, too. I kick my ankles raw as I walk, trying to keep up with her hastened pace. Her agitation seeps through her tight grip on my hand. Her eyes are sad, looking toward something that seems to never come. She sleeps in my room lately; her muffled cries rock me to sleep at night.

We reach the iron gates. The security guard greets us with a lazy nod as we enter the premises. Mother sighs with relief and lets me go. I look for the monstrous, gray bubble, but I don't see it.

I give Mother a confused look, but she doesn't seem to notice. She doesn't seem to notice much, lately. I contemplate throwing a tantrum, but get distracted by the wide-open pool staring me in the face. The bubble is gone. The enchanting display of the glittering sunlight on the pool's surface draws me in.

I look for Peter. I spot his head bobbing in and out of the water, gasping for air in between attempts at a freestyle stroke. He looks funny. Unnatural. Mother sees him too and smiles. No longer her captive, I am free to venture closer to the edge. I watch Peter with jealous enthusiasm.

His coach floats next to him, seemingly annoyed and bored. He grabs Peter's hair and pulls him forward, giving him the needed momentum. He accelerates and succeeds at getting his arm out of the water to take a full stroke.

I watch his progress and smile at his triumph, envious. The coach repeats the same process, kid after kid, pulling hair after hair. I want to be one of them.

The coach looks at me and I feel myself blush. He notices my eagerness and smiles at me, which I take as an invitation. I lunge.

My heart goes nuts with excitement as I hit the water. I submerge, pulled down by my shoes and clothes, fascinated with the bubbles that pass me like giant jellyfish, rushing to the top.

I feel a strong tug, and with disappointment, I watch the bottom disappear. I emerge inches from the coach's stern face. He tows me to the edge and deposits me in front of my pacing mother. He doesn't say anything, but when I catch his eyes, I see the glint of a smile.

Mother grabs me, ignoring the fact that I am getting her soaking wet. I don't need to look at her to know that she is shocked and boiling with anger. But I don't care.

I laugh out loud.

* * *

2012
Boston, USA

I was running late to my appointment. I glanced briefly at the box adorning the top shelf of my apartment before walking out the door, wondering about its possible contents for the first time without a twinge of pain.

You were born to swim, Ollie. Stick with it and it will lead you to a whole new world.

My grandma used to say those words when she picked me up from school to take me to practice. And with childish naiveté, I believed that one day I might just conquer the world, and I would do it by swimming to the top.

It's been two years since Nagyi passed. Sitting down at my appointment, I thought of her box again, letting the mystery of its contents cloud over the pain of loss.

Susan's impenetrable blue eyes scrutinized my face. She hadn't said a word, but somehow the look in her eyes brought me back to the present. Her face showed genuine interest, which made me wonder… was she really interested? I mean, for $120 an hour, I could feign interest in just about anything.

At first I was frustrated that I'd let Kate talk me into going to a shrink. Even the word *shrink* bothered me. Shrinking what?

I looked at Susan dubiously as she sat like a magnificent statue – devoid of problems, devoid of emotions, and supposedly leading me to the epiphany that my life was nothing extraordinary, but quite simply ordinary.

As I sat there thinking of Nagyi, I couldn't help but feel annoyed for having succumbed to all the Freudian mumbo jumbo that my dysfunctional childhood upbringing was the sole reason for my dysfunctional life.

"Olive?" Susan interrupted my reverie, staring at me as if my jumbled thoughts were on display. Her graying flat hair suited her statuesque poise.

I wondered if she was capable of experiencing emotion. An apathetic shrink. I smiled at the irony. Her searching eyes made me feel like a little schoolgirl who had just got caught cheating. My face burned with embarrassment.

Susan's notebook was carefully laid out on her lap, her pen ready on cue. I desperately wanted to know what she was writing in it. I tried to think back to my college psychology classes. Was it attachment or borderline disorder that I would be boxed into? Americans love categorizing.

My mind was jumping from one irrational thought to another. I wanted to go home. The loud clicks of the wall clock marked the crawling time with mocking condescension.

"Hmm, convictions," I said, fidgeting uncomfortably in my seat, glancing back and forth between the ticking secondhand and Susan's probing gaze. I was relieved when her attention returned to her notebook.

"They are a paradox, at best," I continued more to myself than to my eager audience. "Convictions carry commitment and absolute determination to follow through no matter what. Convictions, like getting up one day and knowing that the country where you were born holds no future for you."

Where did that notion come from? I've always wondered.

"And once you made the decision," I blubbered on, "bypassing the nagging logical fallacy of hindsight being 20-20, 'cause you don't get that luxury beforehand, only the unyielding faith that your decision was the right one – you must follow through and face the consequences regardless of how dire they might be," I finished with one breath.

When I walked out of Susan's office, I was none the wiser. I didn't feel liberated, I didn't have any answers, and I was just as confused as before. What were the consequences of leaving Hungary at seventeen?

I've been seeing Susan for a month now, but walking away today, I lacked the conviction that I'd ever get answers. As I walked, my attention drifted to my impending trip to Guam, a tiny island in the Pacific that I didn't even know existed, let alone it being a US territory.

I needed an out – something to do, somewhere to go, or darkness would have swallowed me whole. Which is why, two weeks ago, I'd called Kate.

Chapter 2

1985
Budapest, Hungary

I'm getting my Bluebook today with the official stamp marking me a member of the Ferencvarosi Torna Club. If it were possible to die of happiness, today would be the day.

I am standing in front of the brand new gate. My heart is pounding like crazy, and I want to scream with excitement. It takes tremendous effort to compose myself.

I greet the security guy cheerfully through his office window. He barely glances up from his paperwork to give me a stern nod in return, but his dog runs up to me and wags his tail in greeting. He is not really a security dog.

I walk slowly, savoring the moment, even though I've been coming here every day for almost a year. But I am official today, I tell myself over and over again. I'll soon have the Bluebook to prove it. I feel like I can fly.

I pass the gate with confident steps. I look at the almost-completed complex with newfound pride. As I walk toward the pool, I take a mental note of each building, each field, and each monumental structure.

To my right, there is a two-storied hotel being built to host visiting athletes. There is an Olympic-sized gymnastic stadium behind it, sheltered from view. We occasionally sneak in there to play on the oversized trampolines that are surrounded by a pool filled with giant bricks of foam. Picturing the stadium, I swallow the embarrassing memory of smacking my head in the corner of a trampoline in front of Igor, who I have a major crush on. Luckily, the foam swallowed me whole.

I keep walking, diverting my attention to the other side where a cemented handball court lies, lined with bleachers. Behind the wooden bleachers, there is a football field surrounded by trees – a perfect place for hide and seek. Unfortunately, the field is covered in reddish-rubber turf rather than grass, and it sticks in your skin when you fall. I still feel the burn on my knees from a recent incident.

To my right, there is another football field with real grass, always freshly mowed, and in the mornings, covered in crystal dew. The white goals at each end of the field stare at each other, vacant and lonely.

I keep walking, undeterred, following the curving, paved road. I am close enough to see the first window-covered corridor of the main building that snakes into the belly of the structure – a labyrinth of hallways leading to the pool.

I turn the corner, only to reach another long row of wooden bleachers that semi-shelters the sight of yet another football field. It is *the* football field that hosts most major games; although, the pros play at the *real* stadium about five kilometers from here.

And through the magic doors, I enter the main building that holds the pool… along with an indoor track-and-field turf, weight room, doctor's office, multitudes of locker rooms (some still under construction), and an Olympic-sized handball court.

My heart aches with happiness. FTC is one the most prominent clubs in the country, and now with brand new facilities. I am official. Not only that, but I am one of the chosen ones, selected to train with Dr. S., the Head Coach and Director of the Swimming Program's team.

I am happy.

* * *

2012

Logan Airport, Boston, USA

I hated flying. I was terrified of flying. As the plane headed out to the runway, my hands became clammy from squeezing the seat-handles in desperation.

The plane accelerated. The plane lifted. My body got sucked into the seat. My hands went numb from strangling the handles. Fear and adrenaline commingled in the pit of my stomach and my heart was pounding in my throat.

We were airborne. The sense of insignificance hummed deep in my bones, in synchrony with the engines of the magnificent machine that engulfed me, like a slightly out of tune symphony that's unnoticeable to the untrained ears. Yet, I was the out-of-tune player, separated from the rest by an ill tone of dissonance.

The nagging feeling of being out of place had kept my soul in discord and pushed me to lead a life of insignificance: the silent terror of the mundane. Part of me craved the white picket fence with mini-mes running around in a lush back yard, and a romanticized husband who'd rescue me from my tumultuous mind and ground me to earth.

I can't remember when guilt became a permanent part of my existence. The Catholics would have had a field day with me. And yet, guilt had shaped my life. Guilt for leaving my country, for not being a better daughter, better sister, better athlete, for wanting more, and not giving more.

I'd romanticized life, yet knew not how to live it. I wanted to leave a legacy as much as I wanted to secure a meaningful existence. The incongruity of reality and fantasy left me disgruntled.

Everywhere I looked, I saw hallmark versions of perfect couples, yet deep down, beyond the façade, all I saw was the cheater, the drunk, the self-loather, the pill popper – each wanting more from life and succumbing to their ineptitude, digging their own grave of insignificance.

When did I become such a cynic? The question drew me back to my last session with Susan, the shrink…

"I chase after fantasies," I confessed.

"Like moving across the country for a guy and forfeiting an amazing career opportunity?" she asked, yet her tone carried no judgment. She looked at me with gentleness, but I couldn't shake off the feeling of being mocked.

"If you have to phrase it that way..." I hid my shame with a shrug of indifference. "Call me a romantic?" I forced a smile.

"I tend to live in a fantasy world," I admitted while scrutinizing a dark patch on the carpet, finding comfort in its shapeless form. "And when things don't turn out like I'd envisioned, I get crushed."

"It's difficult for anyone to live up to an idea, Olive. You cannot blame people for not turning out to be what you wanted them to be, nor can you look to them for validation."

Susan sounded too much like my grandma, tearing up old wounds. 'It's time to let go of your demons,' Nagyi'd said.

"It's easy for you to sit there and talk about it as if resolving my issues were the simplest thing in the world. But actually facing them... that's harder," I retorted defensively.

"As the saying goes, insanity is doing the same thing over and over, expecting different results," Susan offered calmly, giving me a slight wink. "Then again, I would be out of a job if that wasn't the case."

She tried to alleviate my frustration by cracking a joke I didn't think she was capable of; regardless, her words struck deep.

"My entire life I've been a slave to routine. Hours and hours in the pool, expecting a different result. Why should it be considered insanity doing the same in life?"

I could tell by her blank expression that she didn't have an answer. She sat expectantly, waiting for me to continue.

"I chase ideas, I agree." Her silence worked. "I am compensating...?" I meant it to be a statement, but it came out like a question.

"You want to be loved, for you do not love yourself," she said, cutting in.

I wondered if that clichéd statement was a required line for all therapists.

"I was unhappy," I admitted, ignoring her last comment, "so I packed my car and left California. Simple as that."

"It's never that simple. You quit your job and a few days later, you drove across the country with a car full of your belongings... for a guy."

"'The best laid plans leave us nothing but grief and pain for promised joy,' right?" I smiled, but she ignored my literary wit.

"You are angry, because this guy shattered your fantasy."

"You make it sound so dramatic," I rolled my eyes at her. "Yes. He. Did. Like every single relationship I've had, I failed at this one, too."

"If relationships were easy, I wouldn't have a job." Susan smiled again, pointing out the obvious.

I had to give it to her; she was trying to be funny.

"But we are not here to discuss relationships with others."

"Aren't we?" I thought that was what therapy was for… as much as it was a prerequisite of being part of the American culture.

"We are here to discuss the most important relationship: the one with yourself," Susan said pointedly.

I thought about the time Matt had shattered my fantasy. I was waiting for him in his apartment with my dignity hanging by a thread and knowing that it would never be the same and yet, obsessing with the possibility that it might.

It was just like my marriage – with Matt, too, I was living a lie. I was living his life, waiting for him to make me happy. Such a burden should have never been placed on any single person. Yet, I desperately wanted to make it work. But the fantasy I'd created, he shattered in his farewell: 'Fuck off'. He'd said it so casually, but with a hint of a condescending smile that lingered on his lips too long to go unnoticed. His words had hurt, but the real stinger was his distrust.

He was possessive, but in some bizarre ways, I'd craved his possessiveness. It made me feel wanted. I'd wanted to be a possession as much as I'd wanted independence – the contradiction tore at me.

When Matt's email had arrived, 'terminating our relationship' as he put it, anger drove me to his office. My cousin always mocked me for my impulsiveness. She always said that I was one of the strongest, most hardheaded, and confident women she had ever known, but when it came to men, I didn't have a drop of self-confidence, let alone self-control.

I was shaking when I'd walked into his office, having no idea what I would say. He'd looked disheveled and stunned when he saw me.

"You scared me," he'd said in such an angry tone that he might as well have said, "What the fuck are you doing here?"

And what the fuck was I doing there? He was sitting by his computer, hunched over, looking at me with those sad eyes – the eyes of the fourteen year-old boy I'd met so many years ago – eyes that were still poisoned by discontent.

Two weeks later my entire wardrobe was neatly packed and placed on his driveway, down to my 10oz shampoo and fridge magnet. His apartment was locked – a nice symbolic touch that complemented his 'fuck-off' good-bye. I was stranded in a strange state, without a job, without a place to live. If it weren't for my cousin…

"You've got to stop focusing on others' motivation and look inside yourself," Susan said, pulling me back, away from my agonizing thoughts as if reading my mind.

"Your fixation on finding love is your compensation for not loving yourself. You want to be validated so desperately that you make men the object of your obsession and convince yourself that it's love.

"You know those dogs obsessed with fetching sticks? The ones who even throw themselves into frigid water, just to emerge with incessant wheezing and wagging tails, asking for more?"

I nodded yes, unsure if I should be flattered or offended that she was about to compare me to a dog.

"Don't be like those dogs."

She reached out and took my hands in hers. Everything she'd said, I already knew. I just didn't know how to change it.

"The problem is that you value yourself based on what others think of you. It should be the other way around. Your estimation of them should rise if they want you, because only then will they have proven themselves worthy of you."

Susan got up and walked to the bookshelf that covered the entire wall of her office. She turned around as if something had just occurred to her. "Stop waiting around for life to catch up to you. Life isn't something that happens to you. You live it."

She turned to face the shelves again, lost in concentration until she found what she was looking for. She slowly returned to her chair carrying a thin book in her hand.

"The best lessons are often found in children's stories," she said and held up Dr. Seuss's 'Oh, the Places You'll Go'. She sat down and began to flip through the pages. When she found what she was looking for, she handed me the book.

"Read the last part," she said instructively.

I began to read. "All Alone! Whether you like it or not, alone will be something you'll be quite a lot. And when you're alone, there's a very good chance you'll meet things that scare you right out of your pants. But on you will go though the weather be foul, on you will go…"

The plane suddenly dropped, pushing my stomach into my throat, erasing all thoughts of Susan from my mind. I leaned back into the seat and gripped the handles, trying to suppress the rising panic in my chest.

Chapter 3

1986
Budapest, Hungary

I hate goggles. They give me headaches and pinch in the wrong places, which is why I refuse to wear them. But I've been swimming for over an hour and the chlorine is burning my eyes.

"What's the matter?" Dr. S. catches me idling at the wall, furiously rubbing my eyes. His voice, so near, startles me and the knot of fear in my stomach explodes. I can tell he's upset by the tone of his question. I want to throw up.

The stabbing pain in my eyes is awful; the chlorine is stinging like needles, and everything around me is veiled in fog. At this point I am not sure what's worse: the pain in my eyes or Dr. S.'s unwarranted attention.

I feel his eyes on me. I don't need to see him to know his look. I am used to it by now: the questioningly raised eyebrows, flushed cheeks, tightly set lips… the look of irritation. So much worse than punishment.

He beckons me to get out. The cold fear stemming from my bellybutton shoots down my legs in waves. The anticipation of the encounter erases all thoughts from my mind. He looks down at me reproachfully. *I'm sorry*, I want to say, but no words escape my mouth.

The silence grows. He is waiting for me, but the lump in my throat is blocking the way. The silence stretches.

"My eyes burn," I confess, and to my surprise, the words match my voice.

He shakes his head disapprovingly and orders me to get back into the pool and something along the lines of bringing goggles in the future. I am so relieved that I don't even feel my eyes burning anymore.

* * *

2012

Somewhere Across the Pacific Ocean

The flight attendant was squatting down in front of me with genuine concern on his face, untroubled by the continuous bouncing that threw the plane in all directions.

"Ma'am, are you ok?"

I was shaking uncontrollably, my feet on the seat, knees cradled to my chest, tears flowing like a broken faucet down my cheeks. I was borderline hysterical, but not a sound escaped my mouth, though my mind was a stage of well-rehearsed chaos. I reluctantly lifted my head from the protection of my arms and knees and met the flight attendant's calm and curious glance with annoyance.

No, I am not ok! Do I fucking look ok? "Yes, I am fine. Thanks," I offered a weak smile ignoring the raging battle in my head and swallowing my irritation at the flight attendant, whose tranquility regardless of the rampant turbulence was aggravating.

"If you need anything, I'll be right over there," he pointed to the far end of the plane with an engaging smile that lingered a bit longer than necessary.

"I'm fine. Really. Thanks." I pressed the thanks with a hint of condescension, irritated at his ill-timed flirtation.

I put my head back down into my cradled arms and continued my silent prayers, counting the minutes before the two pills of Valium and a shot of Benadryl would finally knock me out.

I don't think I've ever wanted something so desperately – to drive a nonbeliever to pray – an odd gesture, yet gratifying, in itself it carries hope, enough to carry you on.

I couldn't remember where I'd read those lines, but found it comforting as I continued to pray. Eight hours to go before reaching the shores of Guam. Eight long hours trapped within my own mind.

Chapter 4

1987
Budapest, Hungary

We are hunkering behind the wooden podium, watching the road that leads from the gate to the main building. It's a little nook in the first hallway; its original purpose is beyond me, but for us, it's the perfect place to remain undetected: our lookout base.

"He's here!" Igor's voice trembles with anxiety and excitement.

As soon as we spot Dr. S.'s balding head, we are down on our hands and knees. We have learned to be quite dexterous in our getaway routine. This entire side of the hallway is windows from the waist up, presenting the best opportunity to watch his arrival, but at the same time, posing the greatest threat. *Knowing*, we decided, outweighs the risk of getting caught.

The idea of being seen is nearly paralyzing, but fear gives me enough oomph to bolt down the hall on my hands and knees. The next hallway lies perpendicular to the first and is about 80 meters long (super long), leading to the weight room, the indoor track turf, and the handball court. It's usually crowded with waiting parents, but not a soul this early in the morning. We abandon caution and run at full speed, the green linoleum swallowing the echoes of our bare feet.

We reach the end and bolt through the wooden double-doors that lead into a narrow, tiled corridor. They squeal on their hinges as we slam into them at top speed; they groan and wobble as we leave them behind.

The tiles are wet and I slip rounding the corner, smashing straight into the wall. They are not supposed to be wet. I look up at Igor, confused. He hesitates for a moment, shrugs his shoulders in a clear "I don't know or care" fashion, and jumps across the small foot-pool that separates the tiled corridor from the atrium of the swimming pool. Then off he goes, down the red carpet that runs alongside, but several feet lower than the pool.

My knee is bleeding, but I feel nothing at the moment aside from the adrenaline that makes my fingers and toes tingle. Not trusting my agility, I choose to wade through the foot-pool and sprint down the red carpet in pursuit of Igor.

By the time I reach the top of the 15-step staircase that spits me out onto the pool deck, I am completely out of breath. The laughter and chatter halts as soon as they see us, and everyone begins to line up in a hushed hurry.

The group resembles organized chaos. We are lining up in front of the shallow teaching pool that lies adjacent to the 50-meter competition pool, tallest to shortest, with toes in a perfect straight line.

It's Wednesday morning. Dry-land practice and hygiene check (teeth and nails). It's a once a week routine. Dr. S. likes order. He likes marching us around the kiddy pool, conducting various exercises and stretches. I wipe the blood off my knee with my towel and toss it aside, hoping he won't notice.

By the time we see his balding head emerge from the stairs, I'm standing perfectly still, which is quite a feat considering there is a raging storm brewing inside of me.

I am holding my breath, willing my erratic heartbeat to subside. There is that familiar knot of fear and adrenaline twisting inside my stomach. I should be used to it by now…

I am barely aware of Igor's banter to my left, teasing me about my height. He is growing like a weed; not too long ago, he was two spots to my right. He is a great friend and super cute. Distractingly cute. I shake off the thought and continue obsessing with the cramp in my stomach. His teasing does nothing to ease my nerves.

Without much greeting, Dr. S. begins his inspection. He seems pleased by our lineup. I'm holding out my hand, confident at my own cleanliness. Avoiding his attention is the fundamental goal of my daily existence.

"Let me see your thumbs," I hear him say. It takes me a second to realize he is talking to me. I readjust my fingers, extending them in a straight line with all my might.

I feel the sting of the blow before I hear it. My cheek aches where his hand made contact. I taste salty tears. They flow unwilled. I force my thumbs up again, to right the wrong. Dr. S. grumbles that of course I hide the dirtiest ones. Luckily, I pass the teeth check; scrubbing them for five minutes this morning paid off.

As he walks on, I look at my nails, feeling betrayed. The sting is gone, but I sulk at my internal injury. I don't like to be at the receiving end of his disapproval.

My brooding is short lived and I stop chewing on my stubs when Dr. S. reaches Mario. He always picks on Mario. I wonder how long he will last with the team. He is a quiet kid, reserved and shy. He is my best friend, Bianca's little brother.

I don't look, but I know what's coming. Mario steps out on cue and walks over to the drain. His face is bleak. In his hands, a toothbrush and toothpaste: his punishment for continuously failing inspection.

There is a hushed snigger making its way down the line… before I realize it, I am smiling, too.

* * *

2012

Tamuning, Guam, USA

What seemed like an eternity later, I finally arrived in Guam. Feeling completely disheveled, I said one more silent prayer of gratitude before I stepped off the plane – grateful to touch land, grateful for the salty, hot breeze, and for the humidity that instantly made my shirt stick to my skin like wet tissue paper.

Kate's glowing smile and hysterically waving arms welcomed me at the gates. It's been several months since I've seen her, but our reunion made it seem like it was only yesterday. Her eyes were shining with excitement. Her tight, borderline-immodest shorts revealed her toned, athletic legs, and her white tank top augmented her tanned skin.

Kate was a natural beauty – her black, shoulder-length wavy hair only enhanced her smooth, slightly oval chin. Her large charcoal-colored eyes always hinted at a mixture of sexuality and innocence. She was never into enhancing her beauty, and found all that stuff frivolous.

As much as her beauty was a gift, it was also her curse. She was often oblivious, rather naïve about her natural sexiness and it tended to attract the wrong kind of men. She had that air about her that she wasn't troubled by men's inclination of finding comfort in her bed. But knowing her, I knew better. She was an emotional time bomb and I was waiting for the inevitable explosion.

Kate planted a kiss on my cheek and hugged me with delighted enthusiasm.

"For God's sake, why Guam?" I was happy to see her, though exasperated by fatigue.

"It's an homage to your new beginning," she chimed her bubbly reply.

"Homage?" I breathed in the reality of my whereabouts, allowing my frustration to dissipate as we made our way to the baggage claim.

"I've always wanted to use that word," she said, laughing. "Would you prefer the word 'intervention'?"

She grabbed my carry-on and placed it on her shoulder. "It's for the both of us, really," she added sheepishly.

That struck me. If Kate needed a getaway, I knew there was something amiss. Judging by the look she gave me, I didn't press further. I smiled back and shrugged. "Lead the way, Katherine."

She hooked her arm under mine, and we made our way to the parking lot, enjoying each other's company.

"Did he really throw your stuff in his driveway?" Kate broke the silence on the verge of laughter, but only because she knew that levity would ease my pain. She put my bag in the back seat and slammed the door of a flamboyantly red jeep she'd rented for the occasion.

Once on the road, I managed to reply. "Yes, he did. I was turning onto his street when I saw a pile of boxes at the end of his driveway. I was confused, thinking someone must be moving out. That someone turned out to be me," I said, laughing.

"Ouch," Kate exhaled with sympathy.

"But his email before that was even better."

Kate raised her eyebrows questioningly. "Do tell," she nudged.

"It said, and I quote, '*someone from the maintenance department will be there to assist you, promptly at 1 pm.*'" I mimicked his deep voice. We both burst out laughing.

During our drive to the hotel, I was mesmerized by the poorly maintained buildings, the occasional liquor stores, pubs, and run-down motels. I could've sworn I was in one of the low-income suburbs of any average, mainland city.

"How did it go with the maintenance guy?" Kate asked, distracting me from the slight disappointment I felt as I envisioned Guam littered with palm trees and exotic huts.

"I drove there early to avoid that embarrassing encounter," I told her. "But really, there was no need, as my stuff was waiting for me, neatly boxed and wrapped in white trash bags."

"Trash bags?" Kate looked at me, confused.

I shrugged. "I have no idea. Protection from rain, perhaps?"

"Wow! A thoughtful prep school upbringing in the making," Kate added condescendingly.

We both laughed again at the absurdity of the situation, enjoying the rest of the ride in silence. I closed my eyes, exhausted, and let the bitter disappointment of yet another broken relationship fade away.

I thought of Nagyi's box – half the size of a shoebox, meticulously wrapped with tape. My mother had given it to me at the airport on my way back to the US. "I thought you might want this," she'd said with tears in her eyes and a tender hug goodbye. "It's a collection of Nagyi's belongings."

After my appointment with Susan, the shrink, and with Guam on my mind, in a burst of sudden courage, I had gone home and opened it. The two years of accumulated fear and anticipation of its contents had proven to be rather anticlimactic.

The box had contained several childhood pictures of our family together, a silver necklace with a cross medallion –

rather odd, as Nagyi wasn't the religious type – a large collection of her delicious recipes, and her favorite book by Katrin Holland. I'd cradled it to my heart. She'd loved this book about a young girl who, out of desperation, attempted suicide but failed even at that, and through a mysterious chain of events, found love and happiness in a new world.

I'd put the book aside. There had been something else hidden among the pile of keepsakes: an old, worn, leather-bound notebook. A diary perhaps, but I had been too nervous and too distracted by the looming flight to dare open it. I'd shoved it in my carry-on, and it was now burning a hole in my bag as I cradled it on my lap.

"We're here," Kate chimed, pulling into the cemented parking structure of a monstrous building. My disappointment must have shown on my face.

"Have some faith, Olive. Don't judge a book by its cover," she said mockingly, knowing my penchant for reading.

We walked up to the automatic sliding doors, which squeaked with the effort of opening. We had to check our momentum, lest we slam right into them.

"Even the automatic doors are on vacation here?" I smiled at Kate, who laughed my comment off and with determined steps headed straight to the elevator, her contentment evident in her stride.

Our room was on the fourth floor: a two-bedroom apartment with its own kitchen, living room, and balcony. If it weren't for the view of Agana Bay and the tropical weather, I would have refused to believe we were actually on an island in the middle of the Pacific.

"Trust me. This will be great," she said reassuringly and plopped down on the couch.

I joined her, happy to relax. She put her arm around me in a protective and loving embrace. "We have two weeks here and I have a plan."

I laughed. "Of course you do."

She pulled me in and kissed my cheek. "Tomorrow morning, we are off to explore. I have some incredible hikes planned. This place will heal you." She beamed with confidence.

"Just me, Kate?" I asked, but she ignored my question.

"Change and go down to the beach," she instructed. "I am going for a run and will bring us some coffee after."

Run in this heat and humidity? But I knew better than to ask. When Kate set her mind to something, there was no stopping her. She was as obstinate as an ox. Running was therapy for her. It cleared her head and gave her some sense of direction in life. She called herself an endorphin junky – the best natural high. I knew perfectly well what she meant. Swimming was my drug of choice.

Kate stood up and disappeared into one of the bedrooms. I contemplated taking a shower, but it would have defeated the purpose. I walked into the bedroom adjacent to hers.

It was a typical hotel room, rather bland, with a queen bed, a nightstand, a small closet with sliding doors, hideous retro yellow wallpaper, and a generic landscape painting of the island. I didn't bother unpacking. I collapsed on the bed, still in a drug and travel-induced daze. I barely heard Kate's goodbye and the door slamming shut. I looked at my watch: 2 a.m., Boston time. It took a tremendous mental effort to add 14 hours to the time and realize it was 4 p.m. here, the next day. I'd lost 14 hours of my life. I smiled at the thought.

I fished out my bikini from my bag and put it on. I looked at myself in the mirror that was mounted to the closet's sliding door and smirked at the ghostly reflection.

I grabbed a towel from the bathroom, not even bothering with the sunscreen. I almost left the room when the sudden urge hit me. I ran back, unzipped my backpack, and grabbed Nagyi's diary.

Chapter 5

1988
Budapest, Hungary

"To the left." We move in synchrony, obeying the command. It's Wednesday morning. Dryland. Again. We must be an amusing spectacle, lined up behind each other in a perfect straight line (an awkward collection of limbs), tallest to shortest, following Dr. S.'s order.

I glance at the kiddy pool longingly as it lies next to us, untouched. I yearn for its warmth, for a time when we can just hang out without a care in the world.

I am waiting for the 'left' command that would indicate the beginning of the march. I'm about to lift my left leg, but instead, he yells, 'to the left' again. He is testing us. Somebody messed up and turned in the wrong direction. Happens every time. We turn in unison and now face the pool. Dr. S. is to our backs, muttering under his breath. It's going to be one of those days.

"To the right," he bellows in his deep and almost-always angry voice. We turn, like well-trained puppies, facing our original direction.

Dr. S. walks up and down the line, inspecting us, casually playing with his stopwatch, twirling the string until it winds around his little finger, only to unravel it and start over. I flinch at the sight of it. The string has an unpleasant bite when wet.

"Left, right, left, right…" We begin our march around the pool to his steady left-right command. I tug at my swimsuit, because it keeps riding up in the wrong places. Flora steps on my heel; I feel a slight stab of pain, and I nearly smash into Oliver. It takes considerable effort to remain upright.

Flora whispers an apology behind me, but I ignore it. I'm frustrated. I don't want to attract Dr. S.'s attention. I regain my footing and rejoin the rhythmic march.

"Halt!" Dr. S. commands loudly.

We stop immediately. Only half of us made it around the first corner of the pool. Anxiety knots my stomach. It's definitely going to be one of those days. I am waiting for him to call my name, thinking he saw me trip.

It's Flora he picks on. I sigh, relieved. None of us would admit it, but I know all of us are thinking the same thing: 'thank God it's not me.'

I steal a quick glance behind me. Flora has gone completely white, which is no exaggeration, because she is already the whitest person I've ever known. She is actually quite pretty, in an odd way. Her hair is white like snow and it matches her barely visible eyebrows. She doesn't talk much. If it weren't for her unique look, I wouldn't even know she existed.

Some of us are facing the opposite direction, but others, having already made it around the first corner, get a straight-shot view. I catch Igor's gaze, who is now second in line. His lips twitch slightly, giving me the courage to turn around.

Dr. S.'s patience is gone. There is a red glow to his face that enhances his receding hairline and plump facial features: clear signs of his rising temper.

Flora hasn't moved; her face is a mixture of shyness and panic. She is so close that I can feel her trembling. Dr. S. beckons her one more time with a voice you wouldn't dare disobey. She takes a few hesitant steps toward him and stops. Not a good sign.

An ominous silence hangs over us as we wait in anticipation. Dr. S.'s face softens, and I become awestruck by that unexplainable upward curve that lurks at the corner of his lips.

Flora stands alone, no longer part of the line, shrouded in fear. I watch as a small streak of pee appears and drips down her bare legs, down onto the tiles, snaking its way to the closest drain. Our collective gasp breaks the silence.

Dr. S.'s lips are still set in that odd, upward curve. His voice is less severe, but still tinged with contempt as he instructs her to clean up the mess. Flora finally finds her courage and sprints to grab a towel, but instead of cleaning up, she runs off, and disappears down the stairs.

"About-face!" The sudden military command sobers us up instantly. We simultaneously do a 180 and realign ourselves.

"Left, right, left, right..." We continue our rhythmic march.

* * *

2012
Hagatna, Guam, USA

The door at the rear of the hotel opened onto a bleak, cemented porch with stairs leading down to the beach. The tide was receding; otherwise, the stairs would have descended straight into the water. The salty humidity wrapped around me like a shawl as I walked out of the air-conditioned atrium, but the gentle breeze coming of the sea cooled the air to perfection.

The hotel's beach wasn't anything spectacular, but the view of Agana Bay was enchanting. Unable to resist the siren lure of the Philippine Sea, I waded into her turquoise depths. Her power was truly magical as she lulled me deeper with her soft, murmuring lament, conjuring up lines of a poem I thought I had forgotten long ago.

The Sea of Faith
Was once, too, at the full, and round earth's shore
Lay like the folds of a bright girdle furled.
But now I only hear
Its melancholy, long, withdrawing roar,
Retreating, to the breath
Of the night-wind, down the vast edges drear
And naked shingles of the world.

I made my way back to the beach, taking deep breaths of the salty air and letting the mirage of the landscape sink in. I only ventured about 100 yards from the hotel, increasingly aware of the burning weight of the diary in my hand. I laid my towel down on the beach, bemusedly watching the myriads of sand crabs scurry away at my intrusion.

The cover was faded, damaged, and torn at places, but it still had that distinct leathery smell – a mixture of musk and birch, combined with dog-breath. When I opened the book, my grandma's silver necklace fell out. I thought I'd put it back into the box before I left.

I held it up to examine it closer. It was a thin, plain, silver necklace barely longer than my neckline with a small cross medallion. The cross was simple and unadorned, about an inch in size, with a tiny orange-hued stone set in the middle. It must have been a gift; I couldn't envision Nagyi wearing a religious token. I wanted to put it on to feel closer to her, but couldn't shake the feeling of being a hypocrite for wearing it. I put it on the towel and looked at the book once more.

The pages were yellowed; several of them were loose, fall-en out of their binding, and some were even torn in half. On many of the pages, the ink had faded into blurred blue patches, making the words illegible. It was distinctly a diary, though. A nervous pang hit my chest at the possibility that I was holding Nagyi's memories in my hands.

Time had taken its toll on the first few pages; the words had faded, and her memories with them. Time had taken a toll on me, too – spending half my life in a foreign land, the Hungarian words my eyes saw, my brain registered in English.

I was caught between the heritage that had raised me, and the new world that shaped me.

In which one did I belong?

I looked at Nagyi's elaborate handwriting, at the curved, inked letters that contained her life. These stories connected her to this world, connected her to me. She used to say that we existed as long as somebody remembered us.

I wanted to remember.

Chapter 6

1989
Budapest, Hungary

Summer is around the corner. School is out and so are our grades. Fifth grade sucked. Colossally sucked. New school. No friends. I was pulled out from my previous school, the cost of being a member of FTC. This one is closer to the pool, leaving me with more time to train. It's efficient and the teachers are under Dr. S.'s direction. Whatever that means. Nearly all FTC swimmers attend it, and yet, not one of them is in my class. I hate it. I'm the newbie; I stand out like a sore thumb. The athlete. The girl who never hangs around. The girl who looks and acts like a boy. Yup, that's me.

Dr. S's new thing is to check our grades. 'An athlete is a manifestation of body and mind', is his latest doctrine. I turned in my grade book this morning and I've been trying not to think about it all day, but it's been like an itch I cannot scratch. All day, it's been gnawing at me. The anticipation is driving me mad, fueling the infested knot of fear in my belly. I failed him.

The grade book: hateful, little book… filled with terrible grades (What can I say? I have no time for studying), and with all the teachers' comments scribbled in them: *She is undisciplined. She is late to class. She is defiant. Poor attitude…*

I fidget in front of his closed office door with Igor, waiting to be beckoned inside – I taste bile in my mouth. Igor is my sole consolation; he flunked one of his classes, too. He is leaning on the wall, calm as an untouched pool. His feigned composure is annoying.

He is so good-looking, just like his brother Ivan. Their mother is Bulgarian. They are rich and very handsome. Deadly combo. I can tell Igor doesn't want to talk (can't blame him), so I entertain myself by thinking about possible punishments. Then again, I can't hold on to one thought long enough…

There are only five of us left in Dr. S.'s group. I'm one of his favorites, which I am totally banking on today. That 'D' in math will not please him…

I hate school. My alarm goes off at 4:50 every morning. I have to reach the 5:15 a.m. bus, or I won't make it to practice on time. I can't be late. I just can't. Mom cries about it a lot. I can tell she feels sorry for me. It's annoying. She has enough on her plate. She seems to cry all the time now. She tried to stop me from coming today. I threw a fit. She doesn't get it. Not showing up for practice? I can't even entertain the idea.

After morning practice, I go straight to school. The days blur… I do like my head teacher. He teaches history and likes to climb up on his desk and sing a monkey song of sorts about being on top of the world, or something. I don't get it, but he is funny. It beats reciting pointless historical facts –

another thing he is very fond of. Then back to practice, and home by seven. My routine…

"Igor. Come in!" Dr. S. yells through the closed door, yanking me back to the present.

Igor's face contorts and I can see a glimmer of fear in his eyes. It gives me a little satisfaction. I'm not alone. He opens the door timidly and walks through. I am stranded outside. Alone.

I want to eavesdrop, but the office door is white plastic; they would surely see my shadow. I pace up and down instead, reciting the same lines of a poem: *'And here in age-long struggles fell, our best and noblest, dead'.* I don't know why it's stuck in my head...

Then it hits me. Dr. S. was quoting it over and over with that look on his face – that look that makes my stomach twist in pain – as he mentioned Oliver's departure from the team.

It feels like an eternity before the door opens again. Igor walks out. His face is grim. Not a good sign. He walks up to me. He hesitates. He grins.

"He is sending us to get ice cream," he says, still grinning like a loon. My dubious expression betrays me.

"I'm *telling* you," he says defensively, and leans in to plant an unexpected kiss on my lips.

I feel the blood drain from my face. Before I can compose myself, he rounds the corner, and disappears down the stairs. I'm paralyzed by what just happened and catch myself touching my lips, stifling a giggle.

The sound of Dr. S.'s voice beckoning me to come in snaps me out of my fantasy. I hesitate. I knock. I walk through the door.

* * *

2012
Hagatna, Guam, USA

I flipped to a random page of Nagyi's diary. It was dated December 1944. After a few lines, I became lost in the story.

My birthday has come and gone. Still no Balint. The radio is blasting continuous warnings about the approaching Soviet Army. They are marching into Budapest. As if the bombings haven't been enough. We've been cooped up in the basement for days now. Again and again. The place smells... smells of unwashed people and feces. Nauseating. At least it helps with the hunger. Hah!

I desperately need a wash myself, but we are too scared to return to our homes. People are terrified of what's to come. I hear them talk about the Reds: whispers of cruelty, of pillaging, of raping as they make their way into Hungary.

The Germans are on full alert, setting up barricades, ready for the siege. We are running low on supplies. I think the Soviets are planning to starve us into surrender. We even ran out of water. No one is volunteering to get more, though there is a well nearby. Ilonka says we should go... I think she is right.

I tried to make sense of her words, but the context was lost on me. I flipped through the pages. They were inconsistent – missing entries, missing dates. The diary had many blank pages, giving it an unfinished touch of urgency.

Maybe Nagyi wasn't much of a writer, or maybe she just got too caught up in her everyday life. Or maybe she just didn't want to write. I'd never know. Regardless, I was drawn to her words.

I found the earliest legible page:

February 1944

We are huddling in the basement of Ulaszlo building, our designated spot. The entire neighborhood is here. Even Mr. Fazekas. He complains about his rheumatism, nonstop. He's at it even now.

People are scared. But they are always scared. You'd think they would've gotten used to it by now. The sirens are wailing. So is the radio. It's full of warnings of the approaching planes: 'Bombers from Baja... Bombers from Baja'.

It's the American Liberators, I hear people say. Bombing us since Monday, making their way to England from Italy. So we just wait. Listening to the radio has become an important part of our lives. The news is often grim, but you can't trust what you hear, anymore.

Balint's been gone three months, two days, and five hours (not counting), and not a single word. Miss him. Miss his voice. I'm trying to picture him singing in the Opera, one day. Accepted into the Franz Liszt Academy of Music, right before he left. I smile even now as I write it down. Still can't believe the offer. I'm so proud of him. I hope I'd said it enough.

I wonder what will happen to us... to our future plans. I am worried Father won't approve. But he is gone, as well. Mother hasn't been the same since. She is more reserved, withdrawn into her thoughts.

It's been over two months since Father's last letter. Finally, Mother confided in me. She never revealed the full contents of his letters before. She needed to talk it out, I think. She said he was with the Second Army at Don River fighting the Reds. The soldiers don't have enough food and supplies to weather the harsh winter there. They don't even have enough rifles, she said, and have to resort to looting the dead. When she finished, she cried. I haven't seen her cry in a very long time. How she kept it in for this long amazes me.

It's been two years since Father's deployment. I look at his photograph often, memorizing his features so that I won't forget.

I flipped to the next entry:

March 1944

I watched Sofia, my next-door neighbor, being dragged out of her home today. I still can't make sense of the events; watching her being loaded onto an already crowded truck with her mother and brother shook me up more than I'd thought. I knew her as a neighbor, not as a friend. Her father enlisted alongside mine; they were sent to the same regiment. He hasn't been back, either.

Mr. Kelemen tried to intervene, but the Germans were ruthless. He got hurt. Mother helped him up when they left. He was bleeding, so she took him into our house. He stayed for a while talking with Mother. Mr. Kelemen is Father's good friend. He was spared from enlisting due to his age; it didn't hurt having government connections, either. So he became our trusted informant.

Mother asked him lots of questions: mainly the reasons for the German influx of late and the rounding up of people. Mr. Kelemen said the Germans are deporting Jews as punishment. All because of Horthy, he said. Hitler found out he was negotiating with the Americans. He was invited to Austria to meet with Hitler, just as the country was besieged. Operation Margarethe, he called it. No one knew it was coming. They came in overnight, an invasion of German soldiers with guns.

Mr. Kelemen stayed with us for a while, all shaken up. Mother stopped his bleeding and offered him coffee. I wanted to listen more, but she sent me to fetch fresh water. She doesn't like me listening when she asks about Father. As if she could shelter me from the news. But even Mr. Kelemen knew nothing of his whereabouts.

I pretended to leave and hid behind the door. But it wasn't Father they were discussing. They talked about the labor camps. He said the Hungarians are no longer safe from deportations, thanks to Horthy's betrayal. Mother caught me listening, and shooed me out the door, just as Mr. Kelemen started talking about gas chambers.

I was embarrassed by how little I knew about Hungarian history. Lying on the beach of Guam, so far removed from that world, it all felt surreal. Who was this girl? My grandmother? In 1944, she was just 15 years old and yet she sounded like an adult.

I became conscious of Nagyi's necklace on the towel. I picked it up to give it another inspection. The stone in the middle of the medallion blazed like fire in the sunlight. Its simplicity made it beautiful. I wrapped it around my wrist like a bracelet. The stone burned my skin at the touch. I cursed under my breath and snatched the medallion away from my skin reflexively, yet the stone was cold, its luster had faded.

If it weren't for the searing pain and an angry blister appearing on my wrist, I would have thought I imagined the whole thing. I tentatively touched the stone again, but it was cold. Being in the sun, it must have absorbed the heat. I looked at the now-dangling medallion one more time, then returned my attention to the book, ignoring the burning sensation on my wrist.

I was drinking up Nagyi's words. The letters on the page, however, began to blur, and there was a dull ache surfacing behind my eyelids, warning of an oncoming migraine. I used to get migraines as a child – frequent visitors, bringing nausea and unbearable pain. The thought of having one sent chills down my spine.

The letters funneled off the page, and there was nothing but whiteness that pierced my eyes like tiny needles. A blinding pain, worse than a brain freeze, wormed its way deeper into my head. I couldn't breathe. I stood up, shaken, rubbing my temples to soothe the throbbing headache. By the time the pain left me, I was bending over, fighting the surfacing puke that clogged my throat…

I was disoriented and dizzy, like being woken up in the middle of the night unsure of my whereabouts. I straightened up and opened my eyes, hesitant, still fighting the lingering nausea. Two large brown eyes met me. My heart jumped into my throat from the sight. But the illusion did not wane.

A gangly, tired, but fierce-looking young girl was staring straight at me. I gave her a tentative smile, but received no acknowledgement in return. I reached out to touch her, but my hands went straight through her. I must have taken one too many pills on the flight; I was clearly hallucinating.

I looked around, humoring myself. I was no longer on the beach of Guam. I was inside of a building, a cellar perhaps. It was dark, save the single light bulb dangling from the ceiling from a suspiciously unsafe-looking wire. The walls emitted condensation that chilled the air. The place smelled acrid, like an overused outhouse.

People huddled by the far corner of this seemingly confined space, talking in nervous whispers – some whimpering, some crying. The building trembled slightly as a plane passed above, accompanied by quiet moans and sobs.

"We need water, Liz," someone behind me spoke in a hushed, but commanding tone. "The well is only a few blocks from here. The sun is setting. We must go now."

I turned around to face another young girl, one who was a bit shorter, but stronger of build. She wore an expression of similar fortitude, holding two empty buckets, one of which she offered to the girl she called Liz. Her eyes reflected neither hesitation, nor fear.

"I'm ready," replied Liz. Her jaw clenched, and her lips pursed into a straight line of determination. The look in her eyes was a testament that she had already made up her mind, too. They stood facing each other, sheltered by the infallibility of their youth.

The reality of the situation finally hit me, even though it made no sense. My body trembled in shock and disbelief. Liz, short for Elizabeth. The resemblance between my mother and her was unmistakable.

I was looking at my grandmother.

But how was this possible? I followed her gaze as she looked around, her eyes settling on a woman squatting at the wall. She couldn't have been more than 30, yet the h

light, bespoke of hardship

disheveled on her shoulders as s

girl cradling an infant.

Liz's eyes filled with pity and

babe won't live through another nig

the angry tears from her eyes. She too

the stairs. The girl followed right be ... *one*

stopped them. I trailed right behind with ... *eful steps.*

The street was coated with debris and h ... *y smoke. It was difficult to breathe, let alone see anything ahead. The girl was leading the way, sprinting down the street before suddenly halting at a corner. Liz, who followed closely behind, nearly crashed right into her.*

"What?" Liz asked and peered around the wall only to pull back immediately.

"Soldiers." The girl spit out the words with a mixture of excitement and fear. "If they catch us…" she began, but choked on the words.

Liz peered carefully around the corner again. "Not today," she said with a smirk. "They went the other way." And with that, she was off, leading the pack this time.

The place was dilapidated. Not a soul around. The cobblestone street was littered with small craters, which they jumped gracefully without much forethought. The windows on the buildings were shattered and massive bullet holes perforated the walls.

We had only gone two blocks, but it felt like miles. My lungs burned from the smoke and the effort of trying to keep up with the girls. My heart pumped loudly in my ears, blocking out the crunching sound of my feet, though my body felt the shock of each step.

shook and I tripped. I got a glimpse of Liz down. She was lifted into the air by the explosion, a nearby building, and ricocheted onto the cobblestone y hands absorbed most of the shock as I fell; rocks dug deep into y palms, and my chin hit the ground hard. The searing pain was nearly debilitating; the taste of copper flooded my mouth.

With the boost of adrenaline coursing through my body, I managed to get on my hands and knees, determined to get to Liz. Shrapnel blanketed her entire body; it was difficult to tell dirt from blood. She lay there bleeding, unconscious. I was paralyzed by fear and shock and ineptitude; all I could do was watch her, helpless. Her neck and legs got the worst of the hit. The shrapnel pieces were sticking out, like needles from a voodoo doll.

Liz's friend was covered in dust and dirt, but otherwise seemed unhurt. She was already by Liz's side, tearing pieces off her shirt and applying makeshift tourniquets. Tears smeared the dirt on her cheeks as she cursed the explosion under her breath, but her hands moved in deft motion, patching Liz up in a hurry…

"Olive?" I heard my name called and felt a slight tug at my shoulder.

"Olive?" I heard my name again. The pull back to reality was sudden; the sharp stabs behind my eyelids were painful, but fleeting.

"Are you all right?" I heard Kate's voice close by.

I was back on the beach in Guam; the diary lay open on the towel in front of me, the taste of blood lingering in my mouth. I touched my lip; it still felt tender where I bit the flesh. I pulled my hand away, a tiny drop of blood staining my fingertip. I was otherwise intact, save for the irregular, erratic pounding in my chest.

Kate sat down next to me and faced the ocean, holding two cups of coffee in her hands. She was doused in sweat, still wearing her running shorts and top, but she discarded her shoes. She was digging her toes in the sand in contentment.

I could feel her worried glances, waiting for me to say something. My cheeks burned from her inquisitive stare, but shell-shocked by what just happened, I couldn't mutter a word. She turned around and lay down next to me, still gripping the two coffee cups. She leaned over my shoulder and began to read the diary out loud.

"... Ilonka took me to three shelters, but each turned us away. They had no room and no equipment for the surgery that I needed. The fourth one finally took us in. All I remember is waking up bandaged up to my ears and aching all over. There was a soldier next to me in bed, but he didn't make it through the night."

Kate's voice trailed off at the end of the sentence. She gave me an inquisitive look. "Is this the book you mentioned on the phone?" she asked, handing me one of the coffees.

Terrified of repeating the experience I just had, I closed the book quickly. "Yes," I answered with a tremulous voice. "My grandma's diary."

"Can you imagine waking up next to a dead person?" she asked, sipping on her coffee, graciously ignoring my peculiar behavior. "I wonder how long he's been dead."

The incongruity of Kate's question about the dead soldier while lying on the sunny shores of Guam was too much. She continued to bombard me with questions, but I just left them unanswered. Seeing my troubled state, she stopped pestering me any further. She was quite apt at tuning into my emotional state and knew when to stop pushing. I was grateful.

"It's white mocha. Your favorite." She nudged me lovingly with her shoulder as she caught me staring at my coffee, still in a daze. "Two percent milk, loaded with whip cream," she teased.

Seeing my stunned look, she added, "Relax! Just kidding."

I gave her a feeble smile and sipped on my coffee.

"Was this your grandma's, too?" she asked, touching the necklace dangling from my wrist. "May I?"

I took it off and handed it to her. Her eyebrows furrowed and she began to chew on her lower lip in concentration. She looked beautiful even when frowning and covered in sweat and sand. She touched the medallion and let out some contemplative grunts.

"What?" I asked, sounding more annoyed than intended.

"Interesting," she chimed, ignoring my impatience. She was very good at that.

"*'October's child is born for woe, and life's vicissitudes must know, but lay an opal on her breast, and hope will lull those woes to rest.*'" She nearly sang the rhythmic lines.

"What?" I asked. "Born for woe?"

"It's a silly poem."

"I got that much, Kate. But what does it mean?"

"It's just a poem that goes with this birthstone," she said calmly.

The random stuff she knew never ceased to amaze me. "Birthstone?"

"Yes, see?" She dangled the medallion in front of me. "It's a fire stone. Opal for an October child. Opal means a mystery of nature. I take it your grandma was born in October?"

I nodded, taking a deep breath of the salty air. I looked at the stone and tried not to think of Liz's lifeless body covered in blood and shrapnel. She was definitely a mystery of nature.

"It's a beautiful medallion," Kate said again as she sipped her coffee.

I hesitantly touched the stone's now cold surface. My fingers tingled from the contact. I dropped it back into the book, masking my feelings from Kate as much as possible. Could it really be possible? But I dismissed the idea immediately.

I sat up and faced the ocean, wanting to enjoy the lulling crash of the waves and my coffee. Kate joined me, withdrawing into her own melancholic thoughts. The silence stretched.

"What is it, Kate?" I pried, unaccustomed to seeing her like that. She gave me a weak smile and waived my question off.

"Let me tell you a story," she said with her usual beaming voice, the sadness having disappeared from her eyes.

"There was a little girl once who believed she was destined for great adventures. Every night, she dreamed of traveling the world and every morning she vowed that one day, she would see its wonders.

"One morning, however, while playing outside, she found a young sapling tucked away in her backyard. She decided to care for it. The sapling grew and blossomed, and its mysteriousness captivated her.

"Eventually, the sapling grew into a small tree. The girl became convinced that if she nurtured it with her love, it would become the most magnificent tree in the world. The years passed, and her dreams of seeing the world faded away into a small corner of her heart.

"And surely, the tree grew to be magnificent, just as the little girl grew to be a beautiful young woman. Men came to her house vying for her love, enticing her with promises of great adventures. But none of them could rekindle that fading spark in her heart. She would not abandon her tree.

"She found consolation in her treasure and convinced herself that once the tree was full grown, she would climb it and see the world from its heights. But as the tree grew, it became impossible to climb.

"The years continued to pass and the woman became older and lonelier. She spent her time gazing longingly up at her tree. And one morning she found an old, bitter, and lonely woman staring back at her in the mirror. In a fit of bitter resentment, she arranged for the tree to be cut down. That night, she went to sleep dreaming of great adventures and never woke again."

Chapter 7

1989
Budapest, Hungary

I watch my brother swim, marveling at his laziness. He struggles making it down and back – pulls the lane line, lags at the walls, scuba dives to the bottom, pulls the lane line even more.

It's entertaining, but he is treading in dangerous waters. He is four years older than I, but lacks the drive and commitment, which is obvious from his effort, or lack thereof.

He practices earlier; he didn't make it to Dr. S.'s group. Only five of us did, selected to train with the seniors. But we really don't train with them; we just practice at the same time.

Apparently, we are still adjusting – evident from yesterday's practice: 1500 for time. Dr. S. pulled us out at the end. We each received a coconut (one of his favorite punishments), a knuckled fist-punch on the top of the head. We named it coconut; presumably, that's how it would feel if one landed on your head.

We lined up in front of him – a pathetic sight. The familiar tingling of fear shot down from the pit of my stomach to my toes just before the burning pain exploded on my scalp from the crack of his knuckles.

We each received two: one for not knowing why he pulled us out, and one for the misconduct itself: swimming like a funeral procession, he'd said. We got a redo. But we were pulled out again… receiving another round of coconuts. This time, because none of us counted the laps correctly. We repeated the set three more times. We are still learning the dos and don'ts of the "senior" group.

Dr. S.'s arrival snaps me back to my brother's predicament. Like a sixth sense nagging feeling, I know today won't end well. Dr. S. walks toward us with a sly smile, carrying his black attaché-case. He looks official and formidable.

We sit in rows of black foldup benches, like little sheep, waiting for his guidance. He will be lecturing us on the backstroke technique, or so he said this morning. He teaches Kinesiology at the Semmelweis University, where he often takes us as guinea pigs for various blood and stress tests, and brings back innovative techniques that he tries on us.

He is in an odd mood. Half content, half irritated; I never know where the balance will tip. He puts his attaché-case down on the table designated for the coaches, and opens it up to retrieve his stopwatch, which he puts over his head with an elaborate gesture; it hangs loose from his neck, giving him a commanding look.

We greet him with proper formality; he nods in return and walks over to the other coaches. They are all young and temporary – his students from the university. He recruits them. They come and go. So many of them. Can't keep track. Some last longer – the meaner ones, usually.

Not many women. But they are each very pretty. On our last swimming trip, one of them was spotted sneaking out of Dr. S.'s hotel room. Zoli said that when he was called in to speak with Dr. S., there were bloodstains on the bed sheet. But that might just as well have been his wild imagination. Regardless, the news spread and we never saw her on the pool deck again.

Dr. S. notices my brother's ineffective training regimen and beckons him out of the pool. My stomach lurches when I hear my name called. For a second, I think he calls me. Then I remember that he prefers to call us by our surnames when he's angry. I feel relieved. But I also feel queasy about it. Peter and I don't have a close relationship, but it is still weird watching him being reprimanded.

I am fairly certain my brother resents me. Maybe for being a better swimmer, or maybe for getting away with stuff our parents usually punish him for. He definitely resents me… But then again, he seems to resent the whole world lately.

We fight. I know how to push his buttons, and although I hate to admit it, I enjoy it. Well, I don't hate to admit it. I do enjoy it. I am like a volcano, though. When I erupt, there is no stopping the burning lava of my verbal diarrhea. He retaliates by physically overpowering me, throwing books at me, chasing me with knives, slapping me around. I get mad and swear so impressively that it makes nearby adults cringe and blush.

I am used to the physical punishments from Dr. S., so being hit doesn't faze me anymore. It's feeling physically inept to retaliate that drives me to madness. So, I hassle him even more. It's a perpetually vicious cycle.

Peter stands on top of the gutter at the pool's edge, awkward. I can't hear them from where we are sitting, but I recognize the angry flush on Dr. S.'s face. It creeps up from under his shirt, the veins on his neck bulge out, and his face flushes violent red – the color of the lane lines.

I recognize a slight smirk on Peter's face: the one he usually gives me before he strikes. With Dr. S., it's an imminent call for disaster. I am so absorbed watching them that I ignore the whispers around me, each asking pointed questions about my brother.

Peter says something to Dr. S. The blow he receives sends him straight back into the pool. I can't quite understand the conflicting emotions raging within my chest. I know in my gut that Peter will never set foot on the pool deck again.

* * *

2012
Hagatna, Guam, USA

With the combination of jetlag and the unsettling events on the beach, sleep was out of the question. I spent the evening reading online articles about Hungary in World War II, while Kate immersed herself in one of her vampire books on the couch.

I was exhausted, yet invigorated. I wanted to piece together the events in the diary. I called my mom and dad, selfishly disregarding the time difference. They were happy to hear from me and I could tell my interrogation pleased them both – brought me back to them, the lost lamb to her fold.

I didn't want to push my mother too much, tearing open old wounds. My father, however, was a different sort. He enjoyed talking about history, of growing up amid the influx of Soviet communism. He rarely spoke of his personal life, but throughout the years, by bits and pieces, I was able to put together a general idea of him as a child.

His parents got divorced (a trait that clearly ran in our family). His mom moved out, taking his older sister with her, leaving him behind. Looking back, and judging from the rare, obligatory holiday visits to my grandmother and her new husband when I was a child, I didn't think my father forgave her completely for being left behind.

He grew up with my grandfather, whom I had never met and knew nothing about. The only evidence of his existence came in the form of old photographs and the story of his passing – never from my father's lips, though – in the middle of the night, while engaging with a prostitute. While some men romanticized such a death, my father, having lost his that way, did not share the sentiment.

So instead, my father talked of politics, of communism, of being nine years old and watching the '56 Revolution unfold from his rooftop, witnessing the hanging of the so called 'rebels' in the park, where they were left for weeks to serve as an example. My father was my personal history book – an information overload of names and dates, which often made my head buzz, just like this evening.

"After Hitler rose to power," he began with a didactic tone of voice, "the Hungarians sought alliance with Nazi Germany.

"The combination of the Great Depression and Treaty of Trianon – where Hungary lost 72% of her land as a postscript to WWI – left us no other options," he continued.

"For a landlocked country, alliance with Italy and Germany meant trading opportunities. We couldn't refuse that. And, as you know, it didn't end well.

"Hungary convened secret peace talks with the Allied forces, soon after the bombings began. Hitler found out, came in, and toppled our government, while hosting Horthy…"

"Horthy was the Prime Minister then, right?" I interjected.

"Yes. At that time," he said. "Hitler invited him to Austria for talks; meanwhile, he covertly overran the country."

"Operation Margarethe?" I cut him off again. I thought of Nagyi's reference to the events. Dad sounded surprised at my knowledge and laughed, pleased.

"Hitler needed us," he picked up where he'd left off. "Hungary stood between him and his troops in the Balkans.

"To further punish us for colluding with the allies, Hitler ordered the mass deportation of Hungarian Jews to Auschwitz. Almost half of all the Jews killed in Auschwitz were those newly deported Hungarians.

"Soon after the German invasion, the Soviet siege of the city began. Budapest became a fortress. The Soviets came in on foot. They fought by numbers and therefore, suffered the greatest losses. Eventually, the city fell. It was one of the bloodiest battles of the war; a strategic victory for the Allies in their push toward Berlin." Here he paused. I could hear his steady breathing coming through the other end of the line.

"The Soviets deported soldiers and civilians in mass numbers to compensate for their losses. Over half a million Hungarians ended up in prison camps, including your great-grandfather."

"Really?" I asked, dumbstruck.

"Yes. Sanka-Papa spent four years in Crimea. Like him, many were taken as Málenkij Robots…"

"Wait, what? Robots?" I cut him off again, utterly confused.

Father chuckled quietly. "Not those kind of robots." His voice softened through the receiver. "Indentured laborers were called Málenkij Robots. They were to assist in the cleanup efforts, so to speak. Mass labor force was a crucial part of the Soviet system. Some people were sent as far as Siberia to clean up rubble, work construction, farms, railways, and even mines.

"Many didn't return until Stalin's death, around 1953. Those who stayed behind in the city were subjected to starvation, random executions, and rape. It was condoned and justified by the Soviets as a collective punishment."

I stood on the balcony after we said our good-byes, savoring the salty night breeze. I was quite overwhelmed with the amount of information he unloaded on me.

I thought of Sanka-Papa, who lived into his nineties. I could still picture him sitting in his chair, wrapped in stoic silence, chain-smoking his unfiltered Kossuth cigarettes, bestowing me with his occasional toothless smile. What must it have been like, being captured and subjected to four years of prison life in Soviet Crimea?

For a long time, I watched the humming nightlife of the city – a crossroad of ancient culture and modern commerce. Surrounded by contemporary comforts, one forgets the suffering such conveniences were built upon. Even this small island and her indigenous Chamorro people had seen enough misery under the Japanese siege. And here she stood, fattened by the excess of capitalist western civilization, the byproduct of being a US territory.

I finally crawled into bed, compelled by physical and emotional exhaustion. I placed the diary on the nightstand next to me, still shaken by what I'd read earlier. My grandmother's necklace was peeking out of its pages, but I dared not touch it. I turned the lights off and let sleep pull me under.

Chapter 8

1990
Budapest, Hungary

I desperately wish my knees would go numb, but instead they ache with a fierce madness from the cracked tiles of the pool deck where I've been kneeling for I-don't-know-how-long. Dr. S. is sitting next to me in his favorite foldable chair that he makes one of us carry to the pool each practice. He hasn't spoken to me since he made me kneel next to him. He is twirling his stopwatch on his fingers, watching everyone else, but I feel his occasional disapproving look.

I keep my head down. My scalp is still throbbing where he yanked on my hair, just above the ear where it hurts the most. I am miserable. My knees burn. The tiles are digging into my flesh and grinding against bone. I'm trying to ignore the pain, but it doesn't work. I lift my left knee a bit to give it a rest. I do the same with the right.

"Quit fidgeting," he snaps.

The gutter breaks my fall. The back of my neck stings from his slap. I should be upset, but it gives my knees a little break.

I want to quit.

* * *

2012

Haganta, Guam, USA

The murmur of voices and the smell of cigarette smoke jolted me awake…

I was standing in the doorway of a wide, long hallway that resembled an abandoned school. Rows of makeshift beds lined one wall, each separated by enough room for a person to stand. The air smelled strongly of bleach in a vain effort to mask the stench of body fluids and festering wounds.

There were scores of men sitting on the floor, lined up against the wall, still in uniform. Two of them had their heads together, gesticulating in a heated manner, but their argument was hushed as if their voices might attract unwarranted attention. Next to them sat a man, a boy really, with a half-burnt cigarette in his fingers. His face was ashen, sunken in, his body heaving with quiet sobs.

Some were sleeping further down, their heads propped against the wall or fallen to their chests, disquieted, even in their sleep. They were all bandaged, haphazardly wrapped in gauzes or splints, but otherwise intact.

I walked slowly, feeling like an intruder, down the narrow passage in between the men and the beds, but my presence went unnoticed. Yellowing curtains divided the beds – an illusion of privacy that was neither provided, nor needed. There were two occupants in each, in worse shape than those on the floor. I began to feel light-headed from the bleach-fumed decay and painful moans that permeated the room.

On the second to last bed, I found Liz. She looked small, fragile, and vulnerable – a visage that was heartbreakingly familiar.

A young man lay next to her in the same bed. His chest did not rise and fall like Liz's. His face was waxen and emaciated, like a poorly carved, abandoned statue. I wanted to look away, but I couldn't. I was drawn by the morbid curiosity that people often feel when they see death.

The young man's eyes snapped opened and he sprung upright. The sheet fell from his abrupt movement, revealing his crushed chest. I gasped from fright and braced myself on the bedpost. His hollow eyes were penetrating and unforgiving as he stared straight at me. He held his gaunt hand out to me… in it was a ringing cell phone…

I woke up in a sweat, disoriented, and with a pounding headache. My phone was shrieking violently on the nightstand.

Chapter 9

1990
Budapest, Hungary

Dad doesn't let me quit. He says I'd be devastated even if I don't see it now, since I've worked so hard to get to this level. He wants me to give it another shot. It takes some convincing, but I give in. Before the conversation is over, I remind him that he said if I asked again, he'd let me quit.

I get to practice early the next day to hang out with Igor, who decides to chase me around on the pool deck, through the black foldup benches where all the seniors congregate, wearing their uniform green and white robes with the FTC logo embroidered on their chests. They are unperturbed by our childish zeal.

Our 'must-have' gear is lined up at their feet, ready for use: kickboard, pull-buoy, paddles, band, and a can.

Acquiring each takes a series of battles. The kickboard is the easy part (you buy it in a shop), but the pull-buoy is a different matter. You've got to have connections… someone who knows someone who could score a pair of egg-shaped, small plastic buoys with handles on their side. I think they might be anchor or signal buoys (as long as we can get our hands on them, no one really cares). Even though they are not meant for swimming, put together by the handles (tied first with wire, then tape), they make the perfect pull-buoy. Sadly, they often leak, which is why we devised the method of melting straws to seal the holes back up.

Paddles are tricky too. We steal the plastic signs off buses, saw them down into perfect squares and drill two pairs of holes in each for the straps that go around our fingers and wrists. When we use them, the pool turns into a maze of bus routes: mine is Bus 99.

Bands are cut from the inner tube of car tires. They go around our feet when we pull to prevent us from kicking. And the can… the infamous, hated can. Dr. S. makes us use it for backstroke. Placed carefully on the forehead, it helps us improve our balance. Liver-pate can is the best; it's just the right size and weight. It used to be a fun dive-and-fetch game, until Dr. S. got annoyed and attached a series of punishments to the number of drops.

Our chase becomes more furious. I like the attention Igor is giving me. His provocative, vivacious laughter gives me goosebumps and every time he catches me, his eyes glint with flirtatious mischief.

The seniors' stoicism doesn't affect us as we run, slaloming through them, jumping their feet and gear like it's an obstacle course. I grab one of the sitting seniors to slow myself down enough to round the corner when a sharp, stabbing pain shoots up my foot and brings me to a sudden halt.

Igor slams into me with a loud thud, nearly knocking me facedown onto the senior's lap. He is so close; his laughter tickles my neck, awakening a swarm of butterflies within my stomach.

I straighten up, out of breath. The entire team has gone quiet and is now gawking at us like we are circus performers. Igor's eyes swell with surprise. I follow his gaze down my leg. My adrenaline is still pumping from the chase, so I don't feel anything, besides an oddly warm sensation emanating from my foot.

It's his ashen face and sudden intake of breath that frightens me, rather than the pool of blood that I am standing in. A rusty, slightly bent can of liver-pate is chilling in an ever-increasing pool of blood at my feet.

I lift my leg to examine the damage, keeping my balance by hanging onto Igor's shoulder. There is a gaping hole on the bottom of my left foot from which blood is gushing out in a steady pace. The circular patch of skin cut by the can is hanging loosely, swinging back and forth as I teeter unsteadily on one leg.

I suddenly feel dizzy and nauseous. One of the seniors gets up and instructs Igor, who is still staring at me in a daze, to take me to the doctor's office, which I'm realizing with despair is quite a hike through the endless maze of hallways from the pool. I wrap my leg in my towel and hop to the doctor's office with Igor's support.

Instead of being worried, I am actually glad that Dr. S. is not present to witness my mishap. Igor delivers me to the doctor's office. The color rushes back to his cheeks from the exertion. He puts up a fight when the nurse begins to usher him out, but loses the battle with dignity. He bids me an apologetic farewell, steals a kiss that makes my heart pound even faster (if that's possible), and leaves me behind with a wink, giving me the courage to combat this alone.

The nurse deposits me on one of the two beds and closes the curtains around me to shield me from my neighbor, or visa-versa. She cleans my cut and interrogates me about the details of my accident. She listens attentively; her face is completely devoid of any kind of emotion, let alone sympathy, and she shakes her head in disapproval. She declares with monosyllabic phrases that I'll need a tetanus shot.

My courage crumbles. Getting a shot terrifies me more than the injury itself, and I throw up a little in my mouth. She disappears to fetch the vaccine and leaves me to my agony. When the curtain is pulled back again, it's Dr. S. who is staring down at me; I am horrified and relieved at the same time.

Dr. S. doesn't ask what happened; I'm sure he heard it from the seniors, or followed the blood trail leading here. He puts his hand on my leg – a touch of comfort. He confirms that I need a tetanus shot, like he has to confirm all injuries and sickness before we are allowed to have them.

The nurse returns with what seems to me to be an oversized needle. I feel the blood leaving my face and I break down in tears. I desperately gauge Dr. S.'s gaze, taking comfort in his never-ceasing smile. The nurse instructs me to roll to my side. I want to scream, but I bite my lip and squeeze my fists with all my might. The sour taste in my mouth is making me want to throw up again.

The sharp pinch in my butt lasts too long, but finally she tells me she's done. I roll back over, relieved. Dr. S. pats my leg one more time and orders me to go home.

* * *

2012
Cetti Falls, Guam, USA

Kate emerged from her bedroom with dark circles under her eyes. While she was the embodiment of confidence, there was also a genuine kindness, an almost childish naivety in her that drew people in. It was her personality, as much as her sexuality – a terrible combination – that made it easy for anyone to confide in her. She always saw the best in people and I admired her for that. I, on the other hand, saw mostly the bad.

By the startled look on her face, I could tell she didn't expect me to be awake at this hour. "Jet lag," I said, smiling at her apologetically. Her puffy red eyes betrayed her reciprocal smile. I couldn't recall ever seeing her like this. She compartmentalized her feelings too well. I've always wondered when her dam would break and flood her with all the suppressed emotions. She headed straight to the bathroom, her feigned smile turning into a yawn.

A few hours later, we were off *boonie-stomping*. It was Kate's idea to explore the wilderness of Guam. Boonie-stomping, she said, was a local tradition involving the exploration of the island's dense forested areas and waterfalls. Before we left, I'd put Nagyi's necklace back on my wrist, unable to leave it behind. Perhaps it was nostalgia, perhaps mere superstition, but I felt her presence with me while wearing it.

Kate meticulously planned out a four-hour hike that started at Sella Bay viewpoint, followed the trail down to the ocean, hugged the coastline of Abong Beach around Pinay Point, taking us back up through the Cetti River by climbing seven waterfalls. It was a mouthful just to say it. It sounded challenging – a good distraction with one minor detail: I hated heights.

For the first hour, Kate and I descended down to the coastline, wading through the thick-canopied forest with determined strides.

"Why is it called boonie-stomping?" I asked, needing the distraction as much as hoping the question would slow her down.

"It's Philippine," she said. "It refers to areas of wilderness or places that are difficult to access. Hence the word boondocks."

She almost always had an answer; it was a quirky, often irritating habit of hers, which, while I was loath to admit it, I very much loved about her. To my slight disappointment, her speed did not wane.

"These are called Banyan trees," she lectured, pointing out some huge canopied trees among the palms as we passed them on the trail. "The natives believe that the spirits of their ancestors reside within them."

Looking at the massive trees, it didn't seem too farfetched. They looked ancient and mystical and eerie and... Very quiet. Too quiet. I suddenly realized why. I hadn't heard a single bird since we started our hike.

"Is it me, or is it freakishly quiet here?" I asked. "Where are all the birds?"

"Oh… Actually, there are no birds on this island," she admitted. "Back in the day, brown snakes hitchhiked to the island on military transports. Not having any natural predators, they thrived and decimated the bird population."

"That's so sad," I said. And creepy, I thought. "So, just to get this straight… We are hiking through a forest of spirit dwellers infested with snakes," I whined, but Kate just laughed at me.

"Stop being such a girl," she teased, knowing that challenging my femininity would shut me up. It worked.

I was seething inside, though, frustrated that I didn't check for diseases and shots before I'd left. I sighed with embarrassment. After all, I grew up in Hungary during the communist regime, before the world became crazed with organic resources and overzealous precautions of hygiene.

We were almost to the shore when we crossed an old stone bridge straight out of a Colonial Era history book. It was intact and ancient and incongruous with its surroundings.

I looked back to admire the still intact structure, overgrown by grass and palm trees. Given another decade, the foliage would hide the bridge's existence completely. Kate said there were many such bridges hidden around the island, once built by the Spanish to connect the coastal roads.

On the coast, Kate picked up her tempo and led the way with fierce resolve. After a few miles of obstacle hiking over rocks, fallen palm trees, tangles and tangles of stinky seaweed, and giant coconut crabs, she finally stopped at a small estuary.

"I'm pretty sure this is the Cetti River," she said, sounding half-convinced, pointing to a river that zigzagged deep into the forest.

She waded into the river without any hesitation and began sloshing through it. I didn't think she'd meant it literally when she said 'hike up the river'. I should have known better.

In spite of my misgivings, I had no choice but to follow, while suppressing images of all kinds of blood sucking, flesh-eating bacteria crawling through my orifices.

At first, I waded leisurely through the knee-deep shallows, my feet sinking slightly into the muddy bottom. The going here wasn't too difficult, even though I had to shake the muck out of my sandals with each step; I was grateful for my Tevas.

The water eventually deepened, and at an unfortunate moment, I stepped into a hole, completely submerging and learning with quiet desperation that Oakley's did not float. My heart ached for them for the next hour.

As we waded through the perfect-plot-line-for-a-horror-movie river, Kate pointed out the occasional surrounding wildlife: the small, skittish geckos and the larger, black and yellow spotted Monitor Lizards that lay on the rocks, seeking sunbathing spots through the occasional cracks in the canopy.

Kate looked back at me triumphantly and pointed to the trees as we passed by. "Those are not seed pods, you know, hanging from the trees…" she began, swallowing a giggle.

"Oh yeah?" I was waiting for the punch line, foreshadowed by her pretentious giggle.

"Those are the infamous brown snakes." She grinned, waiting for my reaction. I just shook my head at her, ready to cry on the inside.

But what could you do, in the middle of nowhere, on an inland, in the midst of a jungle? I stared at the myriads of bamboos covering the banks; some hung over the river, giving it a 'middle earth' vibe. I was ready for a distraction and walked over to one that, over the years, was bent low enough to reach. I grabbed the tree with both hands, determined to cradle it with my feet, ready to make a sloth joke.

"Kate," I yelled to get her attention. "Let's see how strong bamboo is."

"Olive, that bamboo is dead and dry and it won't…"

With a thunderous crack, the bamboo snapped, drowning out her voice. The river swallowed me into her depths and pulled me under with a sucking whoosh. I felt the air rush out of my mouth and nose as I laughed at my stupidity. I sank deeper, pulled by the force of my fall and my backpack. I hit the muddy bottom and bounced with a quiet thud.

Before I was able to push myself back to the surface, the water around me compressed, pressing on my sinuses and temples. I felt darkness descend on me. I opened my eyes instinctively; the urge to see was stronger than my fear of the presumably bacteria infested water. Instead of the murky water, I saw Liz…

She stood before me like an image reflected off a vintage movie projector: grainy and two-dimensional. But it was definitely Liz. She was in a small hallway of a broken-down apartment, standing in a doorway.

She no longer bore the signs of her injury, save for the few light scars that decorated her neck and forehead. She was wearing pants and a man's shirt that was a couple of sizes too big for her. Her hands were covered in flour that she absentmindedly wiped on her pants, leaving white smudges behind.

Her cheeks were flushed. Her chest rose as she took a deep breath and let out an audible sigh. Her relief was obvious. Even her body eased into a calm posture, though she hadn't moved an inch.

I followed her gaze. On the other side of the door stood a man: tall, with thick, black hair that showed hints of curls. It was haphazardly combed, clearly done in haste.

His bundle, no bigger than a backpack, sat beside him on the ground. Pain and suffering carved fine lines around his eyes, yet they shined with youthfulness and warmth. The skin on his cheeks sagged, like someone who had to skip his meals on a regular basis. He might have been handsome, but his thinness and tattered appearance aged him.

They stood, lost in each other's gaze. She was about to say something when, with a determined step forward, he scooped her off the floor into his arms…

I broke the surface with a big gulp of air and heard Kate's hysterical laughter.

"I was about to say," she forced her words out between hiccups of laughter, "that it wouldn't hold your weight."

"So much for the legendary strength of bamboo," I retorted in a failed attempt at regaining my poise.

"Not when it's dead," she said, still laughing.

I marched ahead, mumbling under my breath, suppressing a bitter laugh. Water dripped into my eyes as a haughty reminder of my folly. I refused to acknowledge the vision I saw under the water, and pretended that my sulkiness was due to my wounded pride. Which was partly true. I almost failed to notice that the stone of the necklace, which dangled from my wrist, possessed a fiery glow.

In no time, Kate caught up to me. She smiled at me innocently and began to walk beside me. The water became shallower, only knee deep. We were ascending more rapidly, climbing through rocks and debris, carried and piled by the water during the rainy season.

"Talk to me Kate, and don't pretend you don't know what I'm talking about," I said, ready to divert the attention to her for a change.

She shrugged and waived me off, tears of defiance welling up in her eyes.

"You do attract the damaged ones, you know," I said with an apologetic sigh.

Men, even though she denied it, controlled her life in unhealthy ways. The 'commitment-phobes', I called them. They all wanted one thing: to feel better about themselves at Kate's expense. Men who had no confidence, no self-respect, no ambition, just idling in their lives, flew to her like moths to the flame. Except, it was Kate who ended up being burned, having to hide behind her wall of indifference.

"I don't know what you're talking about," she said in another attempt to blow me off.

"Let me refresh your memory, then," I said scornfully, "starting with your high school sweetheart."

He wasn't really a high school sweetheart. I called him that to get a reaction out of Kate. And judging by the look she just gave me, it worked.

They knew each other back in high school, and (thanks to Facebook), he tracked her down some ten years later. He used the sob story of marrying the wrong girl, wrote love letters about his missed opportunities, and sent endearing text messages.

Charming. Almost. He actually got Kate on the pretense of going through a divorce. She fell for a guy in distress. And it all went to hell. He ended up borrowing money from her, and being so naïve and caring, she gave him a large portion of her savings.

"He never paid you back, did he?" I asked. Kate gave me an angry look. Clearly my question upset her. She shook her head, and looked away from me, embarrassed.

"What a douchebag," I mumbled under my breath, trying not to let my anger get the better of me.

"He needed it to pay his mortgage," Kate retorted defensively.

"He never got divorced, did he?" But I knew the answer even before I'd asked.

"He knocked her up," she said. Her voice was matter-of-fact, without any hint of resentment.

I, on the other hand, was boiling with anger and knew better than to say something that I would have regretted later. But, I would have loved to hear his excuses: *Oh, honey, I cheated on you while we were supposedly going through a divorce. But please don't fret about it. My mistress paid our delinquent mortgage.*

"How about the guy who worked in Admissions?" I asked scornfully, driving the point home.

"What about him?" Kate gave me a sidelong furious glance. I knew I was opening up old wounds, but felt empowered by taking apart her life for a change. And I enjoyed eliciting any kind of emotion out of her, even if it was anger and it was targeted at me. Maybe I was hoping to burst her dam and see her vulnerable, even if just this once.

"What about him?" I imitated Kate's tone of annoyed disbelief. "Let me see. Hmm. What was wrong with him…?"

I drew out the silence for dramatic effect. "Well, he did immerse himself in his job, working and living with prepubescent boys, and only feeling self-assured when in their presence. His opinion was that women, especially *you*, were subservient; meanwhile, he compensated for his emotional cavity by popping Ritalin and anti-depressants."

"Should I keep going?" I took a sip of water from my CamelBak, not nearly finished with my rant.

"Kate, he was an emotional pre-pubescent himself who had no idea what he wanted from life, besides feeling sorry for himself and dragging you into his always doubting and questioning misery."

I knew I was way out of line and judged the guy unfairly. It was easier to dissect people and paint them in a horrid light when they weren't there to defend themselves. But still. I hated how he looked down on Kate (who was accomplished, cultured, and educated), just because she was a woman. He never made an effort to see her, and always made her drop everything to accommodate his life, his time, his needs. He even told her once how he was more experienced, more accomplished than she'd ever be at any job. According to him, Kate simply wasn't "pedigree" material.

"He wasn't good for me," Kate finally cut in defensively. "I know that."

I thought that was an understatement.

"The problem was," she began with a serious tone, "I brought out the ugly in him. And I never understood why."

I couldn't quite believe what I was hearing. "That's not possible, Kate."

She gave me a look filled with such deep sadness that it hurt my heart. He left a deep scar behind; that was obvious. We hiked side by side for a while, taking in our surroundings, deep in our own thoughts.

"And then, there was Charlie…" I broke the silence.

She gave me a slight shrug at that. "I guess I needed a rebound to make myself feel better."

"Bullshit!" I said, catching her in her lie.

"He had some issues, didn't he?" she added with a smile. Even if it was mostly an insincere smile, I was glad for it.

"That, he did," I said, trying not to sound too cheeky. "I hate him the most," I said flat out.

"Why?" She gave me a genuinely surprised look.

"Because he spent months weaseling his way into your life, telling you that you were the *most wonderful, most amazing woman in the world*. But he was just looking for validation in someone younger and found the gullible you.

"Meanwhile, he was in denial that he had problems. And after eight months, he just dropped you without any explanation – on your birthday, mind you – and crawled back to his ex," I spewed, peeved.

"That takes some balls, Katharine. And from your stories, he had plenty of that!"

Her eyes widened in shock, but then she started laughing. I joined her.

"He had a lot going on," she said defensively, but I could tell she was hurt, really hurt.

"They all did…" I pointed it out, exasperated.

"You better not think of him fondly!" I stopped walking and grabbed her by the arm. "Any of them!"

"I am not!" Her voice was defensive. She was definitely lying.

"He never apologized, did he?" I asked, curious. Not that it made any difference.

"Not in so many words," she said, shaking her head dejectedly.

"I feel foolish. I didn't see that coming, you know. I really thought he was… different," she said. Her voice quivered with disappointment.

"You would've been the other woman. You know that, right?" I said, but she avoided my eyes.

"Kate, look at me!" I said, forcing her to make eye contact. "You deserve so much better than that!"

Charlie had issues he needed to resolve. Drinking and dating a middle-aged mother of four was just the tip of the iceberg. Not that anything was wrong with dating an older woman. It was hard to say who needed whom the most: an emotional wreck who nearly lost everything in his life due to his addiction, or a mother of four who was left to raise the kids on her own. Would Charlie qualify as a fifth dependent? But I kept those thoughts to myself. The story made my stomach twist in pain. I felt sorry for him and I truly hoped he'd find happiness in his life, but I was glad Kate was no longer involved in that mess.

"You know, Ollie," Kate stopped and looked straight into my eyes. "I know you can't tell, but they all get to me. Every single one." Her lips curled and her eyes got shiny. The dam was finally breaking.

I don't know why I wanted it to break so badly. For some reason, I was convinced it was healthier to let the emotions out than keep them in, and perhaps because I saw myself in Kate.

"It's not being alone that scares me," she said dejectedly as she walked on. "It's the loneliness that comes from being with the wrong person that terrifies me the most."

I thought hard on that. For me, it was loving someone for the wrong reasons. But I kept that to myself.

After two hours of wading through the river, we'd arrived at the first and (according to Kate), the largest of the seven waterfalls. It was at least 80-feet high and 10-feet wide. The water fell with a steady gush in the middle, ending in a circular pool.

I headed straight into the middle of it to wash away all the muck and sweat that stuck to me like glue, along with the rising panic in my chest of having to climb that monstrosity. The water was waist deep and soothingly cold.

I looked up at the downpour and saw no possible access to the top. Kate, reading my mind as usual, pointed to a makeshift rope that dangled at the far side of the fall, just at the edge of the forest.

"No fucking way, Kate." I shook my head vehemently at her.

"Come on, Olive. I really don't see any other option." She gave me a wicked smile, a cunning retaliation for my prying, and left me brooding in the pool. She walked to the rope, and tugged at it with a grin to reassure me of its strength. I was not reassured.

I followed her reluctantly. The rope looked old. Thick, but old. About every three feet, it had a knot tied in it to help with the climb. From the bottom where we stood, there was no telling where the rope was attached, and no telling how long it had been there, rotting. I looked and couldn't even see where the cliff ended as it curved slightly inland. It was terrifying.

"The key," Kate began, "is to hold the rope with both hands and use the knots to stabilize yourself. Find the cracks in the rock with your feet and use the rope to climb."

Her instructions made no sense. Her idea was to rappel upward, but every fiber in my body wanted to rebel at the thought.

"Okay, if I hold the rope with both hands, how am I going to grab the rocks?" No way was I about to trust that rope.

"By pulling yourself up with the rope," Kate said as if to say, *duh*. And without waiting for any more protest, she began to climb the rope, leaving me behind, boiling with frustration.

The climb wasn't physically challenging, but it took a mental toll on me. Trusting the rope was difficult. Halfway up, my legs began to shake from the excessive adrenaline my body was pumping out. I kept one hand on the rock, disobeying everything Kate had told me. Fuck the rope.

While climbing, my mind was in constant tumult. It conjured up my father's friend who lost his son in a climbing accident. Perfect timing. The story came to me with a sudden flash – how he was using a rope to pull his friend up a cliff without securing himself, how his friend slipped, pulling both of them to their deaths.

I paused to take a deep breath. I heard Kate yell, but I didn't register her words. My thoughts were in complete disarray. I wasn't afraid of falling, but I was afraid. The meaning of Kate's story on the beach finally struck me: what happens to a dream deferred? *They dry up like a raisin in the sun…* I snorted out loud, amused by my lame literary reference as I swayed back and forth on the rope, sagging like a heavy load.

I climbed on thinking of a book I'd just read: of an artist who became bitter and disillusioned from life's rejections and disappointments. His biggest fear was being trapped in a room with a drooling beast whose mind had been eaten out. The beast was humanity and he was helpless to fight back. Was I strong enough to fight such a beast?

At the top, I collapsed on a rock, exhausted, my muscles fatigued by the exertion. I looked up to see the next fall, but thankfully, it looked less ominous.

Kate sat down next to me. "One down, six more to go," she said, amused.

"Sorry for being an ass," I said, still shaking.

She gave me a warm smile in return. She could have thrown my failed marriage or my devotion to a man I thought I loved because he fell in love with me as a 14-year-old boy in my face, but she didn't. She was the bigger person.

"I thought a lot about your story… the one you told me on the beach," I offered in conciliation. "I get it now," I said, caressing Nagyi's necklace absentmindedly.

"I don't want to grow old only to realize that I have not yet lived," I said, more to myself than to Kate. I was greeted by a genuine smile when I looked up at her.

"Now it's my turn to tell you a story," I said. She smiled as if she had expected it.

"Two firefighters go into a forest to put out a small fire. When their task is complete, they go to a small stream. One of the firefighter's faces is covered in soot, but the other one is clean. Which one of them will wash his face?" I looked at her in anticipation.

Kate gave me a slight shrug. "Rationally, I'd say the one with soot on his face, but I know you too well," she said, laughing. "So most likely, it will be the one with the clean face." A sly smile lingered on her lips when she finished.

She half ruined my story, but I laughed, regardless. I didn't mind. "Yes, the one with the clean face. But, why?"

Kate shrugged, waiting patiently for the punchline.

"Because when the soot-covered firefighter looks at the clean one, he thinks his face is clean, too. And when the clean firefighter looks at the soot-covered one, he thinks his face is just as dirty, so he decides to wash it."

"That makes sense," Kate said, deep in thought. "So what's your point?"

"Fair enough," I continued. "In one of his books, Paulo Coelho uses this story to explain his character's relationships.

In your case, the men you fall for see your lovely, clean face and become empowered and confident by seeing themselves reflected in you. On the other hand, you see the soot on their faces, disregarding your beauty, your intelligence, and your confidence and you believe that you are not worthy."

Kate didn't say anything. We spent nearly an hour sitting on the top of the waterfall, absorbing the view and enjoying our silence.

"Look around, Olive!" Her voice was gentle when she spoke, her gaze on the horizon. "These are the moments that make me happy to be alive."

The rolling green, lush ridges that marked our ascent ended in the turquoise blue ocean that painted the horizon as far as the eye could see. The ocean melted into a lighter shade of blue sky where the sunrays intermittently seeped through the patches of white, fluffy clouds. Kate was right. In that moment, I truly felt alive.

"It is magical," I said.

Tears welled up in Kate's eyes, the type that emanated deep from her soul. In the middle of the Pacific, on an island, on top of a waterfall, miles from civilization, surrounded by one of nature's most magnificent creations, human grief caught up to her.

Chapter 10

1990
Budapest, Hungary

I quit.

* * *

2012
Hagatna, Guam, USA

We got back to the hotel around 4pm, completely exhausted. I devoured an entire large pizza by myself. I felt like a stuffed elephant, but couldn't care less.

The combination of mental fatigue and physical exertion left me numb. In dire need of solitude, and feeling terrible for scrutinizing Kate, I excused myself. Weighed down with guilt, I took the diary and headed down to the beach.

I found a secluded spot a short distance from the hotel and tucked myself under a palm tree, appreciating the little shade it provided in the blazing afternoon heat. When I got tired of feeling sorry for myself, I opened the diary and continued reading.

February 1945

The siege is over, but Budapest lies in ruins. Mother said the bridges are gone. Demolished. We are completely cut off from Pest.

The factory is still running. Gun production doesn't stop with the war. But Mother doesn't let me go back to work. "Not yet," is her famous line, even though we desperately need the money. "You haven't healed completely," she says, but really, she is worried about what's happening on the streets. As if I don't know...

She, on the other hand, goes to work every day - war or not, she says, people need their houses and clothes cleaned. Lately she's been accepting food as payment, which is great considering the shortage.

People are hungry and desperate, living off of snow. Mother said people have even butchered the horse carcasses on the streets. The bakeries are on rations, too. They are using everything they can find to make ends meet. Mother found a mouse inside one, baked completely through. Luckily, she only showed it to me afterwards. I make our own bread, now.

March 1945

Mother finally let me return to the factory. The Soviets are everywhere, but soldiers are soldiers. Same attitude, different uniforms.

The Reds are more mean-spirited and bitter than the Germans were, however. Their intimidation often ends in violence. They have rounded up many people - no one knows where they take them. Mother says it's for the cleanup efforts, but the streets are just as run-down as before.

Mother paints my face with coal each morning and ties a kerchief on my head to make me look older. She makes me wear her clothes, as well. I look ridiculous. But, she says, the Reds are looking for the pretty ones and this way, she doesn't have to worry.

I was so immersed in reading, I barely noticed the dull pain that began throbbing in my temples… tha-dum - tha-dum, like a drumbeat of a marching troop, getting louder and louder as they approach the battle.

The funnel of letters, blinding whiteness of the empty remaining pages, nausea, disorientation… all too familiar. The transition was less of a shock this time. I braced myself for the impact. When I regained my sight, I was back in Hungary…

I recognized some of the familiar features of Budapest from my childhood: the cobblestoned streets, trash and debris littering the ground, the run-down buildings that survived wars, yet still retained their architectural grandeur. The smell of the city was also all too familiar – a pungent blend of people, smog, cigarette smoke, and stale urine. Unpleasant. Nevertheless, my stomach twisted with homesickness.

I was scanning the faces, trying to find Liz. It took me a while before I recognized her. Her face was smeared in black and the clothes she was wearing aged her significantly. Even the way she walked – stooped, eyes fixed on the ground – reminded me of an older woman. But her eyes, her most unique feature, reflected resolve and courage.

There were many people on the street, busy with their own affairs. She blended in, unnoticed. Soldiers mingled in the crowd; their presence was felt, noticeable by the safe distance people kept from them.

We passed a bakery that was overflowing with people, waiting wearily for their turn. They bulged through the doorway, like a snake that just swallowed its prey, slowly moving down its digestive system, spewing out the rest onto the street, blocking the flow of pedestrians. They stood with heads bowed in morose acquiescence of their fate, their collective grumble of discontent reverberating down the line.

There was an army truck idling nearby, across the street, packed with an unruly group of drunken Soviet soldiers carousing amongst themselves, their youth evident in their beardless faces. Their Russian tongue felt foul on the ears. They were the only ones laughing – a mocking juxtaposition to their battered surroundings. One of them looked in my direction, his lower lip bulging with tobacco, and grinned with crooked, yellowed teeth. He paused in mid-sentence to spit off the truck and wiped his mouth with the back of his hand.

We continued down the street when two more soldiers rounded the corner. Liz carefully stepped aside, edging closer to the wall to keep out of their way, her gaze fixed carefully on the ground. They were also speaking Russian; their voices echoed down the street, loud and unpleasant. One elbowed the other and they stopped in their tracks. Liz stopped and leaned against the wall, afraid.

There was a young woman standing in an alcove, mere steps ahead of us. Like Liz, she wore worn clothes and men's boots. While she was crudely dressed, her youth and beauty was evident in her face. She was the object of their attention.

Liz stepped around the soldiers, keeping her composure as much as she could, but I could tell she was shaken. She pulled into the next alley and leaned against the wall; her rapid breathing betrayed her anxiety. While Liz tried to compose herself, I stepped out of the alley to watch the commotion unfold, driven by curiosity.

By then, the soldiers had over-powered the young woman, forcing her out onto the street. They were laughing and jesting at her expense. The young woman kept her eyes down, shaking her head and muttering under her breath, terrified. She tried a few unsuccessful steps to escape her tormentors, but each time, her attempts were carefully blocked.

No one on the street stopped, cared or dared – it was difficult to tell which. The woman began to cry, which aggravated the soldiers even more. One of them grabbed her chin and spoke provocatively, while the other sized her up with a leer. She tried to pull away, but couldn't escape his grip. When he let go, red fingerprints stained her cheeks. She made several more futile attempts, which only resulted in her losing her coat, and ripping her shirt. Her torn garment hung loose, revealing her bare shoulder. Her face flushed, her hands trembled as she tried in vain to cover herself.

It was difficult to watch the cruelty with which the soldiers treated the young woman. It filled me with range and bitterness as I gripped the corner of the alley, distanced by space and generations.

My heart leapt as an older man with thick, disheveled hair and a strong build stepped out of the bakery line to finally intervene. He walked poised, unperturbed by his ragged appearance, and took off his coat to cover up the young woman, murmuring comforting words to her in the process. The soldiers, however, didn't appreciate his chivalry. One of them struck the man on the side of his head. He fell forward from the blow amid sneering laughter. Dazed and bleeding, he staggered to his feet. If he was afraid, it didn't show.

By now, the commotion had attracted the attention of the soldiers across the street. One by one, they jumped off the truck and approached, like hyenas attracted to the scent of easy prey.

I was so engrossed in the unfolding tragedy that I almost forgot about Liz. I stepped back into the alley to check on her, but she was gone. In a panic, I ran down the street, away from the scene. I was relieved when I caught up to her a block away. She was walking with a quickened pace, her arms crossed tightly across her chest. I looked back over my shoulder several times, hoping to catch a glimpse of the conflict unfolding behind me, but was thwarted as we rounded the next corner.

We'd walked several blocks when two shots rang though the street. The sound echoed off the walls and shook my bones to the core. I half-crouched to cover my head, thinking it was another explosion.

Liz exhaled a little shriek, but she kept her composure, otherwise. I saw no smoke, no debris, only people hurrying by on their way as if nothing out of the ordinary had just happened. The look of sudden comprehension on Liz's face must have mirrored my own as the fate of the young woman and her rescuer dawned upon us…

I was jerked back to the beach so abruptly that I barely had the time to turn my head and throw up in the sand. My throat burned, barely masking the blistering pain of the necklace against my wrist.

Chapter 11

1991
Budapest, Hungary

I am back at FTC, my hiatus having lasted less than a year. I took up rowing with my cousin, who is the reigning national champion. Her love of the sport was infectious and I desperately needed an out: no fear, no pressure, supportive coaches, and great friends. But it wasn't swimming. It was fun, but without swimming, I felt like I'd lost a limb.

I was hesitant returning to the club, but my father's good friend (who happened to be one of the coaches), showed up at our house unannounced to convince my father that I should return to the sport.

I was ambushed. He spent an hour telling me that I would be a waste of talent if I'd stayed away, making promises left and right, ensuring me that he would be my coach. While I haven't forgotten the time his flip-flop bounced off my head in the pool for failing to learn the breaststroke pullout the way he wanted it, he actually got to me. I made the leap to come back, only to find out he'd lied.

Coming back sucked.

The club is infested with newcomers. While I was gone, one of the nearby clubs had shut down and FTC inherited their coaches and swimmers alike. Most of them are very fast and, of course, they now swim with Dr. S. The senior team has nearly quadrupled in size. They are his new prodigies, his new favorites.

The club is now a constant buzz of noise. I feel like an outsider. I am an outsider. I get the treatment of a rookie, and yet, ironically, it's been six years since I walked through these doors.

Dr. S. walks by me, every day, without a glance. He doesn't acknowledge my greetings. He doesn't acknowledge me at all. I would be lying if I said it didn't faze me. I am no longer in his group; I lost all the privileges of being a favorite.

As punishment, I have a new coach: Lacika. He is in his twenties, handsome, and to die for. I am in love. Swimming for Lacika is like dying and going straight to heaven. He doesn't hit us. He, too, pushes me beyond my limits but I love it. If he is my punishment for quitting, it was so worth it.

I can't think about our trip to Luxemburg without it stirring up butterflies in my stomach. The bus ride took us almost 24 hours. I fell asleep spread out on two seats, only to be woken up in the middle of the night by Lacika's gentle caressing. I was confused, groggy with sleep, and yet so comfortable in his arms. I wanted him to keep holding me. He smiled at me and shushed me back to sleep. It was one of the happiest moments of my life. Has it been a dream? His warm smiles says no. It makes no difference; I've been fantasizing about him ever since. If only…

Needless to say, I won every single event.

Since Bianca quit, following her brother, Mario, I have a new best friend: Niki. She came from the other club as well and swims with the seniors, but I don't hold it against her. She is 14. Two years older than I.

She is in love, too. His name is Karesz, also from the other club. He coaches the little ones, so he spends most of his days in the kiddie pool. I think he is too old, but Niki says, he is only 37. He seems really nice; though, I only see him in the pool, lifting weights, or sneaking around with Niki. They try to keep it on the down low, but everybody knows. Nothing stays a secret. That much hasn't changed around here.

I ask her how it was losing her virginity. She giggles when I ask; she's been bubbly ever since. It happened in the coaches' office, she says, and dives into details that make me blush, which is not an easy feat. I swallow my jealousy with great difficulty. I am but a stick: all legs and no chest. I wouldn't find me attractive, either.

There is only one way I can think of to make Lacika notice me: by swimming. Swimming fast.

* * *

2012

Apra Harbor, Guam, USA

For the past few days, I'd put aside the book and allowed myself to clear my head, and really give myself over to the island. We'd spent our days learning to scuba dive, exploring the island, and discovering more about the indigenous Chamorro people. It didn't take long before I fell in love with Guam.

Scuba diving, as it happened, was one of the best decisions of my life. Within three days of training, we were allowed to dive off shore. Kate decided we must explore Apra Harbor on the western side of the island.

Apra Harbor was formed by the Orote Peninsula and the low-lying coral reef of Cabras Island. The peninsula was like a thick, fat thumb about to pinch a bug with its long, skinny Cabras forefinger. It was a magnificent natural harbor that provided safe waters, and it was deep enough for large ships to anchor. Hence, its tumultuous naval history.

Today, the US Navy sat on its southern part and claimed the peninsula for its base. As we boated into the harbor, we were like tiny ants crawling along a giant mammoth of an aircraft carrier.

Diving in Apra Harbor was like exploring a haunted house. It was a historical graveyard where two warships had sunk almost on top of each other during two different wars, and lay trapped for eternity.

The visibility was poor, the water murky, but peaceful and warm. We were descending into hallowed ground, slowly, following the midsection of the Tokai Maru's hull until we reached the Cormoran.

The SMS Cormoran was the first to succumb to its fate. The German warship, originally designed for the Russians as a passenger-cargo freighter, was downed by her own crew in

1917. The ship anchored in Guam for two years under US friendship, for the US was neither participating in the war, nor was it inclined to provide coal for the Germans to sail on.

Unfortunately for the Germans, the US eventually joined in the war and planned on commandeering the warship. The warning shot fired at the Cormoran was the first shot fired by the US in World War I. The Germans, however, had another plan: blowing up the ship rather than handing it over, sacrificing nine of their own in the process.

On the other hand, the Tokai Maru was a Japanese warship hiding in the harbor before following the Cormoran to her grave in 1943. It was nearly 150-feet larger than its German counterpart and took a set of US torpedoes to sink.

Submerging into this graveyard was like exploring the darkest parts of my soul. Breathing under water was as exhilarating as it was gratifying – I was at one with the water. My lungs expanded with each breath, rushing the oxygen-enriched air to my extremities, calling my muscles to action. It was the purest form of meditation, where two planes of existence collided.

I was thousands of miles away from both of my homes, under the sea, hidden from the world, where two empty shells of warships lay buried – skeletons of their previous lives, but skeletons that still whispered the song of young men fighting in senseless wars, brother against brother, in a world that only a few remembered still. Their souls drifted under the water among the ruins of these two ships.

At 100 feet below, the keel of the Tokai Maru met the rudder of the Cormoran. I was floating in between the two empty shells – *no light but rather darkness visible* – one hand on each when the water turned black…

Rationally, I knew I was deep under water. I was aware of my surroundings – not by sight, but by a deeper consciousness. I felt the chill of the water on my skin, the pull of the tank on my back, the smooth, forlorn shells of the tankers under my palms, the regulator in my mouth, and the pinch of the scuba mask on my face.

With each intake of breath, the compressed air rushed through the regulator with deep Darth Vader-like vibrations. I had to concentrate to slow my heart rate and keep my breathing even. I knew what was coming and didn't want to hyperventilate under these circumstances.

Light suddenly penetrated the darkness, burning through my scrunched-up eyelids, leaving blotchy spots in its wake. I kept reminding myself that I was floating in between the two tankers, but when I finally regained my sight, I beheld an entirely different vision.

I was in a hallway with halogen lights mounted to the ceiling that dimmed and brightened like the pulse of a slow-beating heart, offering glimpses of the weathered walls. The cracked lime green paint revealed the gray, water-damaged concrete beneath. The chairs and equipment that decorated the hallway were also corroded by time.

It took a moment before it sank in: I was in a hospital. The distinct bleach smell that masked the ammonia stink of urine and leftover cigarette smoke trailing the people who passed by was an instant link to my childhood memories.

I walked down the hallway into a small examination room, drawn by the sound of chocking sobs. There, I found Liz. She was older, in her early twenties, but distinctly her. A little girl, no more than four, was clinging desperately to her legs; her curls hung loose and disheveled, half covering her flushed face. She stared straight up at me as if she could see me, her eyes dark and accusatory. I was frozen with the realization that the little girl was my mother. I looked at Liz; her attention was focused on a solitary bed where a little boy was turning red from wheezing, barely able to breathe through his hiccupping sobs.

A nurse was hovering around the doctor, following each of his instructions with an expression of detached indifference. The doctor talked fast; it was difficult to follow. The few words I caught were: high fever, water-filled lungs, aspiration.

When the nurse presented him with an oversized needle, my knees buckled. I wasn't reassured by the hygiene of the place, let alone the competency of this doctor as he was waiving around the needle like it was a mighty sword.

The shock of realizing he was about to use the needle to drain fluids from the little boy's lungs made me want to scream, but only a gurgling sound escaped my mouth.

While I was nearly hysterical, Liz stood as composed as a Greek statue of a pissed-off goddess, and refused to leave the room. The doctor didn't argue, and the nurse continued to remain indifferent; she merely closed the curtains around the bed to shelter them from view.

The boy's cries eventually faded away; I presumed from being anesthetized. I took the opportunity to compose myself and look around. We were definitely not in Budapest. While hospitals in the city would never match up to Western standards, the poverty and lack of care of this place were beneath even Hungarian standards.

The curtains were drawn with urgency. Liz's terrified gasp pulled me away from the little girl's probing gaze. The doctor appeared, cradling the boy in his arms. He stepped through the door with haste and disappeared down the hallway, the boy's limp arms bouncing with each step. Liz ran after him, half pulling, half dragging the little girl behind.

I was seized by a sense of dread that clutches the heart and squeezes it hard enough to steal your breath away. I took a hurried step toward the door, but it dissolved into darkness. I was stuck.

Something latched onto my leg, pulling me back with a powerful force. The floor was disappearing underneath me, and I was sinking into its soft ground, unable to move. The room faded away into nothingness. I panicked, kicking and flailing helplessly…

I was back in the water; my shallow breaths through the regulator were making me light-headed. The glowing stone of the necklace swayed limply, casting an eerie glow on my surroundings. There were no warships in sight. My brain was in flight mode and all I could think of was getting to the surface. I needed air, real air. I began to kick hard, my fins propelling me upwards.

The tug at my leg became stronger, pulling me back with force. I now registered it as Kate, but my urge to reach the top, to breathe fresh air, was overpowering my senses.

For a few seconds it was a tug-of-war: I wanting to reach the surface, she determined to keep me under. She grabbed one of my fins and yanked it off to stall me further. She grabbed me with both hands and shook me until I gave in and finally stopped.

When I realized the stupidity of my actions, I completely surrendered to her. She was frantically groping at my BCD, looking for the air-release valve. She wanted to keep me under.

She leveled us at 15 feet. It took her confused, alarmed look before my brain adjusted and all the warning instructions of decompressing before surfacing finally hit me. Without proper stops, especially diving to 100 feet deep, the nitrogen could form bubbles in the body, causing serious damage, called decompression sickness.

Kate gave me a frightened look. *You need to pass gas!* Her favorite scuba phrase popped into my head and made me smile, but I'm sure it came out like an insane grin through the regulator.

Chapter 12

1992
Budapest, Hungary

"Ollie, Dr. S. wants to see you in the gym," Ginger says, entering the locker room in her gym clothes. Her tone is somewhat defensive and she gives me a look that says 'don't shoot the messenger', but then seeing my shock, she cracks an encouraging smile. I collapse on the bench, halfway undressed. It takes me a moment to compose myself. I look up to press Ginger for answers, but she's already gone.

Ginger is Dr. S.'s protégé. They have a true, symbiotic relationship. I only know what that means, because we just covered it in bio class and, surprisingly, I was in attendance. I got a warning that if I missed any more days, I'd have to repeat 8th grade, which is funny, since I exceeded the yearly-allotted absences a long time ago. The upside of being an athlete is getting away with shit.

Though Dr. S. makes Ginger weigh in every week and mocks her relentlessly for being "overweight", she still gets the most attention. In return, she is Olympics-bound.

Dr. S. is adamant about his swimmers maintaining proper weight. At least Ginger's weigh-in routine is private; others, aren't that lucky. Katalin (another potential, though less favored) gets the grunt of his scrutiny; she often hides her tears behind her goggles, especially on days when Dr. S. questions her father's ability to fund her eating habits. Those days, I am thankful for Lacika.

There was a time when eating everything on our plates was a must. 'No essential vitamins should go to waste,' was one of Dr. S.'s favorite edicts. Poor Igor set the perfect lesson for us merely a few years back. We were not to leave the table until he consumed all the green beans off his plate. We watched him with burning empathy only shared misery could evoke, but underneath it all, it was quite an entertaining lunch. The beans, after all, did not settle with him and a few minutes into his conquest, they reappeared on his plate. When the stench of his vomit perfumed the entire restaurant, we were finally excused.

I miss Igor. He followed in my footsteps and quit. We maintained our friendship outside the pool for a while, but it was never the same. Swimming was our connection, which broke the minute we both quit. The strings that held us together now lay severed, unattached. I still feel the phantom tug of the lines, but even that fades, leaving nothing but the silhouettes of our shared memories.

The shock of Dr. S. summoning me unsettles me completely. I look down to realize that I've already changed into my suit. I must have been on autopilot. I continue to linger in the locker room, hoping to avoid the inevitable.

I just came back from a week off, my reward for qualifying and competing at the Cadet European Championships. My only break for the year. I am eager and ready to continue my training with Lacika. Based on our successful season, I feel invincible.

I make my way to the door brooding when Niki bursts through. She kisses me excitedly and bombards me with questions that I can't quite register; my brain is too preoccupied.

An intense, incomprehensible longing masks the growing pang in my stomach. "Have you seen Lacika?" is all I manage. Her face contorts and she stops talking immediately.

"What?" I ask. My voice shakes and my stomach twists into that painful knot of fear that I haven't experienced in nearly two years. "What?" I ask, a bit more forcefully than intended.

"He was fired, Ollie," she says gently, as if lowering her voice would soften the blow.

"He was *what?*" I ask, just to make sure I heard her correctly. "Fired? Why?"

"Stealing money," she says, but I can tell from the look she is giving me that she doesn't buy it.

"Dr. S. wants to see me," I blurt it out with growing dread.

"Why?"

I shake my head and leave the locker room dazed – I barely hear her yelling after me, telling me to find her later.

As I make my way to the gym, I try to think of the events that led up to Lacika's firing. He was assigned to our group; the group Dr. S. didn't want. I assume that's because we lacked the necessary potential.

My first big competition with Lacika was a disaster. He made me swim almost every event as a test of my endurance. Taking nearly a year off had hurt me more than I thought it would.

I was devastated. Lacika pulled me aside and held me until my exhaustion and disappointment-induced sobbing waned a little, and told me through my lingering hick-ups that next year would be different. He said I was born to swim the individual medley and the butterfly; the only events I would swim from now on. His unwavering confidence carried me through another year of grueling training.

The 400 IM was on the first day of Cadet Nationals this year: I came in 5th. It was an ugly swim, though. He didn't say it, but we both knew. I could read the disappointment in his eyes. I was so angry; I refused to end another meet this way.

The 200 Butterfly was the following day – my last chance to make him proud. I finished second, right behind the reigning champion, qualifying for the Cadet European Championships.

He cried.

When we returned to the pool, Dr. S. broke his two-year silence. He cornered me with a big smile, and even hugged me, complimenting me on my swim. My "reward" was training with him for the Championships. Lacika wasn't happy. Neither was I.

It didn't go well…

Walking down the green linoleum hallway feels different now. Each step is laden with bitterness. I hesitate at the entrance to the gym. My hand is shaking as I reach for the handle. I take a deep breath and push the door open with a bit more force than intended. The door squeals on its rusty hinges and slams into the wall behind, announcing my entrance with an obnoxious groan.

Dr. S. is sitting at the desk reading the paper, not even bothering to look up. The gym is empty. The air is thick with sweat and with the metallic odor of overused machines. The thick, rubber stretch-cords mounted to the ceiling are still swaying slightly from recent use, greeting me with their taunting silence, as if knowing that I will be their next victim.

I linger at the door for a while, uncomfortable. Dr. S. finally looks up. "My old fox!" he greets me with a sly smile as he folds the paper with elaborate precision and puts it on the table.

He doesn't get up from the chair, but waits for me to come to him. My heart beats faster with each step. He pulls me to him and embraces me, his hug lasting awkwardly long. He slaps my butt, an indication that I can step back.

He makes a couple of jokes about how I'm his oldest swimmer, the fox, since I've been at the club as long as he. The fact that he calls me 'his' doesn't go unnoticed. Lacika is gone, I remind myself with aching disbelief.

He asks about high school, which I am about to start this fall, but he already knows that, since he'd arranged it. All FTC swimmers attend the same high school. He stands up and walks around the desk. I follow with growing trepidation.

He is talking about a friend of his who just started up a pentathlon club. I have no clue what a pentathlon is and why this is relevant. I know it involves five sports, but that's about the extent of it. I couldn't care less. He hasn't spoken to me this much in all seven years combined.

He doesn't look at me while talking. He is arranging the content of his black attaché-case. He puts his stopwatch inside while he says how unexpected my time was on the 200 Butterfly.

"Not bad for an old fox," he says and snaps the metal locks in place.

He turns around finally and studies me. His eyes are too little for his face, accentuating his now mostly bald head. He's picked up smoking lately and the stench of tobacco sticks to him like gum to your shoe, even though he tries to mask it with an incessant amount of cheap aftershave.

"But let's be serious," he says.

The light from the high windows catches his face and I notice beads of sweat on his forehead. He leans on the table and crosses his arms over his slightly pudgy stomach.

"In the next few years, you might drop a few more seconds," he continues with an offhanded tone. "But realistically, that will be the extent of your swimming career. You won't amount to anything in this sport."

The muscles on his jaw twitch slightly as he delivers his sentence. His sentencing. For a moment, I forget to breathe.

"As I was saying, my friend is looking for athletes for his club and I think you'd be a good asset to his team."

His words sink in. He means it as a compliment. I think. Doesn't he? I hug my chest, hoping it will restrain my confusion, my trembling body. If I am not a swimmer, what am I?

The calm façade I'd put on crumbles. "Swimming is my life," I exclaim with a barely audible shriek. I can no longer contain my shock. I break down in tears.

Dr. S. grabs his attaché-case, pats me on the butt, and leaves me in the empty gym.

* * *

2012
Hagatna, Guam, USA

After the scuba diving fiasco, we decided to take it easy the next day. It was still early in the morning, but the heat was already unbearable. I was sitting outside on the balcony that still provided some shade, overlooking the Philippine Sea. The view was both serene and somber.

Kate followed me out and sat in a chair next to me. She handed me an iced coffee; I gave her a grateful smile. She leaned back in her chair with a content sigh, and stretched her legs out on the railing.

"What happened to you yesterday?" she asked, without looking at me.

I told her everything: about the diary, the headaches, and the visions. She listened without interruption. When I came to my underwater fiasco and the little boy in the hospital, she gave me an inquisitive look.

I thrust my arm under her nose and wiggled my wrist at her dubiously, Nagyi's necklace swaying back and forth. "I, uh… think this necklace has magical powers," I said, trying not to sound too stupid.

She grabbed my wrist, steading my slightly trembling arm, and examined the stone one more time. Whether she believed me or not, she didn't say.

"If we are at the point of psychoanalyzing each other," she said with a serious tone, throwing my arm back at me playfully, "I think reading your grandma's diary might help you come to terms with your own past." She raised her eyebrows at me as if waiting for a rebuke.

"You might be right."

She was rather taken aback by my response, clearly anticipating an argument. She leaned back in her chair and closed her eyes.

"You are right, too," she said, after a prolonged silence.

"About?"

"Everything you said yesterday. About me getting involved with the wrong men."

She took a deep breath, ready to get something off her chest. "I slept with my neighbor," she said, nonchalant.

She caught me by surprise; that wasn't what I'd expected. I shook my head in disbelief, glad that her eyes were still closed.

"He said he loved me," she said with a quiet chuckle, but her voice was thick with condescension.

"What happened?" I asked, but I knew my question was irrelevant.

"He loved weed more."

Her punchline was so unexpected and absurd that I laughed out loud. She smirked and closed her eyes again. Her lips were pursed, curved slightly downward with a hint of smugness that told me that she was slightly amused by this short affair.

She was such an incredible woman: intelligent, sexy, independent, and funny… I caught myself sounding like an online dating profile. She was ensnared in the web of finding love in the 21st century. We both were. And it was an unforgiving place to old souls like us.

"We are trapped in a world of electronic love," Kate said sullenly, as if reading my mind.

She opened her eyes and stared longingly at the sea. "Intimacy is nothing more than a sequence of emojis, butchered grammar, and snaps of edited images." She sighed, her bitterness hanging heavy in the air.

"We measure love on social media – shiny, happy, perfect lives plastered over two-dimensional lies. Where everything has a price. Where success means expensive labels. Where perfection is defined by the absence of blemishes, absence of body fat, absence of hair, duckface selfies, oversized tits, and a Kardashian ass," she said, laughing sardonically.

"Yes baby, I love it when you objectify me," she said, feigning a satisfied moan.

She looked at me, her eyes shining with tears of disappointment. "People don't want to settle down, Ollie. Look at all the options. It's like a grocery store full of people vying to be bought. Swipe left, yes, swipe right, no. Swipe, swipe, swipe…" She moved her index finger left and right in the air mimicking swiping on a tablet. "It's window shopping for sex. Intimacy? What's that? Face-to-face conversation? Nonsense."

I could tell half of this conversation was taking place in her head, and needed to be let out. I sat there patiently, waiting for her to finish. Ranting like this, though quite rare, was her way to forgive herself for being foolish. I quite enjoyed them; it was a sign, an emotional breakthrough, letting me know that she'd be back to her old self in no time.

She took a deep breath, still looking at the sea. "'Bae, check out my ride. It's a 750LI. Let me snap a pic of it. Hey Versace, meet Gucci. I've got 600 followers and it just keeps growing. Hold on, one more selfie. Another bottle of Dom Perignon? Girl, that's how I roll. See my gold? But hold on, let me flex this joint and get real loud – it's business time.'" She paused to let out a bitter laugh. "'But let's get real, bae. I lead a hood life. For you, I ain't got no time. So I'm out. You can find your way home, right?'"

She turned to me again, her eyes now glinting with amusement. I smiled to myself; the spell was broken. She was fine.

"Did you know *bae* is a Danish word for shit?" she asked, catching me off guard by addressing me directly.

"What?" I asked, momentarily lost.

"*Bae*… the word people incessantly and interchangeably use on social media for babe. It's Danish… means shit," she said, again, emphasizing on shit.

"Shit?" I asked, baffled.

"Yup. Poop, crap, turd, feces, excrement…"

We both laughed, long and hard. Time stretched as we sat there, lulled by the lament of the crashing waves.

"I take it the little boy died?" Kate asked, shattering our melancholic silence.

It took me a moment to understand her question. "He must have," I said, crestfallen.

"Perhaps you should call your mother," she suggested.

She was right. I walked into the apartment, leaving Kate on the balcony. I welcomed the air-conditioned chill after the stifling heat. Disregarding the time difference yet again, I selfishly called my mother. She picked up with a tired, sleepy voice; she always slept with the phone next to her, in case I called.

It made me wonder if I'd ever love someone that unconditionally; if I would ever have a child. I never knew what people meant when they claimed their biological clock was ticking. Now that I've reached my mid-thirties, the nagging feeling that I was getting too old weighed on my mind like a broken faucet that you don't notice at first, but eventually the drip, drip, dripping drives you mad.

I chitchatted with her about Guam for a few minutes, intending to let her wake up a bit before diving into more serious matters. But I couldn't hold my curiosity any longer; without further preamble, I asked her about the little boy. I could tell she was surprised, but she offered up her story without hesitation.

"Balint, my little brother, was born when I was two," she said, her voice sounding distant. "He was a sweet little thing, as much as I can remember…"

"He got sick, didn't he?" I asked, cutting in impatiently.

"Yes," she replied, unfazed by my rude interruption. "When he was about two years old. He had a really bad case of influenza, but Mom was convinced it was TB."

"Tuberculosis? Why?"

"My dad returned from the war very weak and in poor health. He contracted TB soon after. Even though he was treated and recovered completely, Mom always blamed him for passing it on to Balint.

"The infection spread to his lungs. There was no time to go into the city. The doctor in town, however, wasn't a specialist. He attempted to drain the fluids, but pierced his lung instead. Balint suffocated within minutes."

I barely registered the rest of our conversation. I was stunned by the story. "Have you told me this before?" I asked, trying to make sense of my latest vision.

There was a long pause on the other side of the receiver. "I don't know," she said softly. "I might have."

After our goodbyes and promises of calling again soon, I went back out onto the balcony. Kate hadn't moved an inch.

"I couldn't fathom losing a child, let alone by a mistake that could have been avoided," Kate said after I recounted my mother's story.

"It's fascinating how the mind copes with pain," she said softly. "Sleep offers a comfortable distance, and with time comes forgetting," she said and grew quiet. "Then, there is death…"

"Death as coping?" I asked, laughing. "You are so morbid… Perhaps a happier option?"

"There is madness," she said with a jest, her eyes still closed. "Some say it's a preferable alternative to reality."

"I choose forgetting, then. Time heals all wounds, right?" I said, still laughing at her gruesomeness. "Plus, living is much preferable to dying."

She cracked her eyes open and gave me a sheepish smile. "Here is to forgetting, Ollie," she said, raising her nearly empty cup of coffee in salute. She took a sip and closed her eyes again, smiling to herself.

Chapter 13

1993
Trenton, Italy

Dr. S. has decided to let me stay, and since there is no more Lacika, I've once again been 'promoted' to the senior group. Ever since he pulled me into the gym, part of me wants to quit, while another part wants to prove him wrong.

Training is more grueling, and my migraines are more frequent. I spend too many hours in the pool, plus weights, plus dryland… By the time I get home, I am too exhausted to do any kind of schoolwork. I compensate by smoking cigarettes and sneaking into clubs on the weekends. Freshman year of high school is going by in a blur.

I'm in Italy right now with the Junior National team. I am fairly certain Dr. S. sent me to test my loyalties and abilities. His 'do not let me down' still rings in my ears. It's been a lonely trip. The other swimmers all cling to their own clubs, and since I'm the only one from FTC, I am mostly ignored.

It's time to warm up. I feel nervous and exhausted; I'm beginning to doubt that my crumbling willpower will last me through this meet. I manage a couple of hundreds when I know something is off. My arms feel like bricks and there is an unfamiliar fluttering sensation rising from my stomach, all the way to my chest.

I stop at the wall to take a few deep breaths and rid myself of this fluttering. My chest tingles and my heart begins to pound. Fast. I take another deep breath, submerge to the bottom and exhale gradually, focusing on slowing down my heart rate. I come up, breathe, go under, exhale.

It doesn't work.

I look down at my chest; my heart is beating so fast, I can see it through my swimsuit, pushing against the thin fabric as if it's the only barrier keeping my heart confined in its place.

I linger at the wall, confused. Scared. The pool is crowded. I feel so alone. Water splashes in my face each time someone flips at the wall. I hug the lane line to get out of the way.

I search for the pace clock on the wall in desperation. I put two fingers to my neck, trying to locate my pulse, and count the beats for six seconds. Just like we do in practice. I start at zero, counting for six seconds… It's too fast. I almost lose count. Was it 26 or 27? Wait, that's 270 beats per minute. That can't be…

I find my pulse again, starting on the bottom this time. I can't keep up... 28? Times 10, that's 280. I'm on the verge of tears. My heart is a chaotic mass of beats. I check it one more time, but I give up counting when I reach 20 and watch my chest's arrhythmic display instead, fascinated. Freaked out.

I hug the lane line even tighter like it's my lifeline, and wait. Another minute goes by before my heart is back to its steady rhythm. My relief is instantaneous. I take my pulse and count for six seconds: 10. That's 100. I exhale and push off the wall to continue my warm up.

If I just pretend it didn't happen, it will surely go away, I tell myself. I certainly don't want to be labeled as an attention-seeker.

The meet is an absolute bust. I am so embarrassed that I ride the bus home pretending I am not even there.

Dr. S. gives me the cold shoulder when I return to the pool. I'm growing rather fond of his 'you-don't-exist' attitude. My wallowing is short-lived, though. Before I can sneak down the stairs after practice, he beckons me to him and says that if I perform like that again, representing him, he will never send me anywhere.

I sulk away, starting to believe that maybe he is right: I will not amount to anything.

* * *

2012

Hagatna, Guam, USA

I decided to spend the afternoon by the hotel's pool. I dragged one of the sun-chairs to a shaded, secluded spot that still overlooked the sea, and immersed myself in Nagyi's diary.

May 1945

Balint's been blacklisted and with it went his dream of the Opera. He is heartbroken, but hides it well, even from me. But I can tell.

Mother gave him money to get his truck license. The only job he could find that hired ex-soldiers. Even though he'd spent an entire year as a POW in Britain, the Soviets blacklisted him anyway.

It's been months since his return. There is not much in the city for us, but mother doesn't want to leave, hoping Father will return home as well. 'How would he find us if we left?' she often says. Balint gave her hope. Yet, it's been over a year since his last letter.

Balint doesn't talk much about the war, or his captivity. He changes the subject every time I ask. At first, I got upset. We fought. I yelled. I hit...

No reaction. So I stopped asking. He has changed. He doesn't look at me the way he used to; there are days when there is nothing but emptiness in his eyes. He looked devastatingly like a scarecrow when he returned; he must have weighed less than I.

Mother's been hovering around him, making sure he eats plenty. He is still pale and thin; his cheeks are sunken and the dark patches under his eyes seem to be permanent. I try to hover around him too, but he keeps me at a distance.

His mother sold all his belongings, even his clothes. When he came home, he had nothing but his knapsack. He doesn't blame her. I do.

Balint is full of excuses for her. The Soviets stripped them of their family title and seized all their land. His mother is not accustomed to hardship and taking care of herself. Excuses. She has no problem bossing me around whenever we visit, but for Balint's sake, I endure it.

What kind of a mother gives up on her only child? I bite my tongue and keep my thoughts to myself.

I continue working in the factory, while Mother cleans houses, and Balint... if all goes well, he'll be driving trucks.

I flipped through the remaining pages. The entries became more infrequent – missing months, missing years. Many pages contained 'to do' lists and recipes that I first thought were diary notes. It was difficult not to feel disappointed.

August 1946

We got married!

Mother gave her approval, even though we knew Father wouldn't have. Maybe part of her already accepted the inevitable. She signed the underage permission form, and she even gave us money to take the streetcar to the courthouse. She couldn't miss work; we can't afford her being replaced by somebody else.

I felt that familiar jolt of pain behind my eyelids as I finished the sentence. The page blurred. The intense heat emanating from the stone seared the skin on my wrist; I gritted my teeth.

I leaned back in my chair, closed my eyes, and took a deep breath, embracing the oncoming headache. This time around, the trip was slightly less unbearable…

Liz looked beautiful, not yet seventeen and full of life, standing in the doorway of her apartment, wearing a wedding gown. The dress was long, ivory satin, and embroidered with beautiful flower prints. It looked handmade. I wondered if it was her mother's creation.

The intricately woven lace of the sleeves wrapped around her small wrists. The collar was done with the same lace-design, elongating her neck, highlighting her lightly tanned skin. Her hair was pulled back tightly in a bun, bound in a similarly patterned lace-snood.

She did a little twirl in front of Balint, and made a slow, elaborate curtsy, looking coy and mischievous at the same time. She straightened up, laughing. Her sincere and contagious laughter perfumed the air with happiness. Balint lifted her off the ground and swung her round and round the foyer. His hard laugher was muffled when he buried his face into her neck, and danced her around the foyer.

He looked handsome, even though the suit he wore seemed a couple of sizes too big. His hair was combed stylishly to the side. He had a lot more color to him than the last time. Even the dark bags under his eyes faded to a lighter shade of gray. They looked happy, even after everything they'd been through. My heart ached watching them embrace and kiss…

The feeling was fleeting, however: A moment later, I was back in Guam, the taste of salty tears on my lips.

… We found two witnesses at the courthouse to sign the papers. We didn't have the money to take the streetcar home, but we didn't mind. It was a beautiful day; we walked home as husband and wife. Mother stayed at our neighbor's to give us privacy. It was a lovely night.

Chapter 14

1994
Budapest, Hungary

I'm in the bath, delirious from lack of sleep and somewhat incapacitated from the continuous drinking since… yesterday? I think we'd started yesterday. Or the day before.

The music and obnoxious drunk yelling is loud enough to shake the whole house. The bathroom door barely muffles the noise. The water is soothing, almost sobering. Almost.

I close my eyes, lean back in the tub, and try to envision my reunion with my mother. She returns from her trip to Greece in a couple of days and will find her place completely trashed. She left with Nagyi. I think it was a consolation prize for finalizing her divorce. Something like that. She's been living in this house for the last year or so.

House… more like a shack with few amenities, really, but it's on an incredible property, laden with amazing fruit trees. Mom made the place quite homey; she added a couple of rooms and insulations so it can bear the winters.

We used to spend our summers here. I'm not sure how we scored this place, considering no one owned anything under the Soviet regime. At least that's what I hear when Father talks politics. Mom is worried she's going to be evicted. Since the Hungarians reclaimed the country, it's becoming increasingly difficult to hold onto "property" that you technically never owned, but used as your home your entire life. Mom can't afford lawyers and the 'new' government wants to reclaim this property; it must worth a shitload of money.

The house is up in the hills, overlooking the city, which lights up gloriously at night, like bright stars reflected over a calm lake. The place is surrounded by untouched and undeveloped land. Even the nearest neighbors are only here a few weeks in the summer. It can be eerie. But I guess that's why Mom got Brutus. He is *my* consolation prize for the divorce: a beautiful, purebred Doberman. Lion King Brutus.

And he loves me.

Guilt sweeps through me for locking him in the shed. His whining doesn't help, reaching me through the bathroom window in spite of the blasting music. But he is too skittish, and intoxicated people are not his favorite playmates. Ever since Peter took him to that weird training camp, he hasn't been the same. He growls at everyone. I hate my brother for it.

I doze off in the tub. Going under jolts me awake. The water has cooled to lukewarm. I turn the hot water on with my toes; the delicious hotness warms me up instantly. I try to recall how I got myself in here. I lean back till the water covers my ears, letting the running faucet block out the outside ruckus.

Time is a blur. I remember Brutus biting Balazs in the face, which is why he is in the shed right now. I remember Miki punching through the living room window and bleeding all over the rug in a fit after an angry encounter with his girlfriend. I remember Dodo breaking my mother's bed jumping on it like an ass. I remember being on the rooftop at one point with Niki and a bottle of peach vodka.

I don't remember getting into the tub.

Mom has no idea that I took over her place to throw a three-day party, and Dad thinks I am spending quality time with Mom. This divorce is working out perfectly for me. I try not to think about the inevitable consequences when she returns. The alcohol and hot water helps with that.

I sit up and turn off the faucet before the bathroom floor floods completely. I grab my glass of OJ and vodka mix that's been flirting with me from the foot of the tub.

Oblivion is preferable to guilt and self-pity. I close my eyes as I sip on my drink, enjoying the warmth and the bass beat that reaches me through the closed door.

* * *

2012

Agat, Guam, USA

Kate decided our next adventure was hiking Mount LamLam. She gave me an impish smile as she outlined her plan. We drove our rental to Stella Bay Viewpoint parking lot, off of Route 2. Well, it was more of a small pull-off area than a lot; the same one where we began our Seven-Falls hike. Mount LamLam lay across the road.

It was crispy hot outside with the taste of salt and a touch of electricity in the air, forewarning of an oncoming storm. Half the sky was blanketed with dark clouds. I voiced my concerns to Kate, but she just laughed it off.

"And each particular hair to stand on end, like quills upon the fretful porpentine," she said with a smirk.

Kate loved quoting literature. I was usually good at figuring out the source, but I was too hot and bothered to think. I teased her with my silence.

"It's Hamlet, Ollie," she blurted, looking disappointed that her reference fell on deaf ears.

"What's a porpentine, anyway?"

"It's a porcupine," she said, with a touch of know-it-all attitude.

"Why can't you just say porcupine, then?" I shook my head in frustration.

"Geeze! It's Shakespeare," she said, and smacked my arm playfully.

"You look ridiculous, you know that?" I mocked her in retaliation.

"Don't tell me I didn't warn you," she said, dismissing my mockery.

She looked like a clown, wearing a long-sleeved shirt and socks that covered her knees. There wasn't an inch of exposed skin on her body.

"'I was seeking for a fool when I found you,'" I grinned at her, proud of my wiseass rebuke. "How is that for Shakespeare?"

"Touché, Ollie, touché." She turned away from me, sizing up the mountain in front of us.

Kate said there was no well-travelled path leading to the top and we would have to bushwhack our way through. It's not that I didn't believe her (well, maybe I didn't), but the 90-plus degree heat and humidity that left my body in a constant pool of sweat didn't really inspire me to bundle up.

I compromised by wearing long, thin tube socks, but that's as far as I was willing to go. I settled on shorts that were barely longer than modesty allowed, a tank top, and a baseball cap. I was still mourning my Oakley's.

The first hill we encountered off the road posed no difficulties. It gave me an opportunity to revel in the striking landscape.

Behind us lay the ocean. The slight breeze to our backs caressed my skin, drying the sweat off my neck. The sun was to our right, bright and blazing like a reigning queen enticing her angry twin of darkness to come and dare to play. Dark clouds were gathering their forces to our left, ready to take on the challenge. In front of us was Mount LamLam, an optical illusion: I could almost touch her, yet between us were miles and miles of crisscrossing emerald peaks and intricately carved valleys.

"That's sword grass?" My jaw dropped when Kate's warning finally made sense.

She saw my expression and laughed. "Yup, that is sword grass," she said with a trace of smugness.

She descended down the hill; I followed in tow, mesmerized. The closer we got to the next hill, the taller the grass seemed, until it towered over us, unfettered.

"Kate, a jumbo shrimp is still a shrimp! This is not grass."

I had envisioned sword grass as pointy, thin grass, perhaps a bit longer than untended weeds in someone's back yard. This was something else. In front of me was a cornfield of thick, leafy, so-called-grass, with edges like a serrated steak knife. Each strand was two inches thick or more, reaching up to at least 10 feet in height. My curiosity got the better of me and I touched one to investigate. The grass sliced through my skin with ease, leaving an instant flow of blood behind. I yelped.

"Don't you dare say, I-told-you-so," I warned Kate, sucking on my bleeding thumb.

She took off her backpack, unzipped it, and tossed a long sleeve shirt at me, grinning in the process. I scowled at her, nursing my cut and my wounded pride.

"So which way are we going?" I asked sulkily, putting on her shirt.

"The shortest distance between A and B is a straight line," Kate said with a pompous air.

There was no straight line and I didn't hesitate to point out the obvious.

"They are connected, see?" I followed her finger as she outlined the rising ridges that snaked up to the top.

The hills and valleys were inter-connected with narrow ridgelines that made me think of the Great Wall of China.

Suspicion took a hold of me. "There must be a path if this place is well-traveled and famous."

Kate's lips twitched mischievously. "It wouldn't be boonie-stomping, now would it?" she said with a wink. "All we have to do is avoid falling into the ravines that you can't see through the grass."

I exhaled my frustration. Kate ignored my pouting and disappeared into the maze of grass. I followed diligently, braced for an epic battle.

Two hours later, battered and bleeding, we made it through the thicket. We encountered a series of rock formations that arched their way to the summit.

"It's limestone," Kate offered, seeing my awed expression.

"Mount LamLam used to be underwater, so much of the mountain is limestone, but you can't really see it because of the lush undergrowth," she said, out of breath.

The storm hadn't caught up to us yet, but now it concealed most of the sky. The yellow rays of the late morning sun struggled to peek through the cumulating storm clouds.

"Just embrace it, Olive. You are almost on the top of the tallest mountain in the world."

I sipped on my now lukewarm water and wiped the sweat off my forehead. I didn't bother asking what she meant, knowing well that an explanation was forthcoming.

"How do you measure a mountain?" she asked as expected while maneuvering around one of the massive boulders.

"From its base?" I replied, rolling my eyes at the seemingly pointless question, trying not to sound patronizing as I followed her around the rock.

"True. But what if you measured it from its deepest point?"

"I don't follow."

"Ok. So listen to this. We are somewhat on top of the Marianas Trench, which is the deepest point of the ocean, right?"

"Sure," I said, entertaining her point.

"That makes this the greatest change in elevation on Earth," she said, triumphant.

"But that's kind of cheating," I pointed out, but she just shrugged in retaliation.

"It's all semantics," she said.

"So how deep is the Trench?" I asked as we began mounting yet another boulder.

"Close to six miles deep," she said speculatively. "If you dropped a pebble into its depths, it would take about 64 minutes to fall."

I sniggered, not quite sold on the facts. "Where did you get that number?" I asked, questioning her accuracy.

"Read it online," she said, shrugging her shoulder.

"It must be true, then," I said, laughing.

She walked on, paying no attention to my sarcasm. Whether her facts were true or not, the depth of Marianas Trench was remarkable.

"What's the elevation here?" I asked. "And I mean from the base, not the ocean floor."

She laughed. "About 1300 feet, I think."

It sounded meager compared to the Trench. She looked back at me just to see my unimpressed expression. She stopped in her tracks and gave me a stern look, just to emphasize her irritation.

"I know, I know," I said, putting up my hands defensively. "It's all semantics."

We continued our battle to the top. Once on the summit, I collapsed on the topmost rock. I unrolled my now soaking wet socks to let my legs breathe. My thighs looked like Edward Scissorhands just had a field day with them.

Kate shook her head. "You are going to love swimming in the ocean after this hike."

I looked toward the ocean with a mild sense of foreboding; I did not want to think of the salt on my fresh cuts.

It was beautiful, though not what I'd expected. Still, it was a consolation prize for my battle wounds. "The bastard child of fantasy," I mumbled under my breath.

Kate made a grunting noise. Apparently she'd heard me. She took off her backpack and joined me on the rock, handing me a Luna bar.

"You know what your problem is?" she asked rather briskly while unwrapping her own. "You focus too much on the destination. Look down. See the road?" She pointed straight down, chewing loudly.

"See the ridges over there that slalom all the way up here?"

"Yup," I said with my mouth full.

"We hiked that," she said with an emphasis. "Now, that's no bastard child, Ollie."

I laughed as she threw my lines back at me. She knew me too well. I looked at the progress we'd made, and she was right. I felt a satiating sense of accomplishment. It was about the journey, as cliché as that was.

Kate pointed to an island off the coast. "That's Cocos Island. It's partly a resort, partly government-owned. They breed native birds there in an effort to reestablish them on the mainland. We will make a trip there on our last day here. I signed us up for the annual Cocos Island swim," she said with a gentle smile, her eyes eager for the challenge.

Cocos Island was rather small. Only a mile long, she said. It seemed far off in the distance from up here, but according to her, it was only two miles offshore. It was narrow, like an index finger, pointing away from the mainland as if saying 'the sea is that way'.

Between the mainland and Cocos Island was a triangular-shaped lagoon situated above a reef, about several miles square. It was an assortment of green and vivid blue, betraying its shallow depths, a striking contrast to the deep darkness of the sea beyond. We sat there quietly for a while finishing our snacks and watching distant lightning strike the sea.

Kate zipped her pack and stood up, ready to go. "We better beat the storm," she warned.

I didn't move. There was a familiar tightness and fluttering rising in my chest. Kate sat back down and regarded me with concern.

"Not yet. I'm about to have an episode," I told her.

She'd experienced them a few times in the past and weathered it a lot worse than I.

"Need to lie down?" she asked with a quivering voice.

"No. That just makes it worse. It won't take long," I reassured her.

And suddenly my heart began to beat with a feverous rhythm. Kate took my wrist to check my pulse, her face turning pale.

"Come now, it's not so bad," I said, laughing. "It will be back to normal in a minute, give or take."

"This is so bizarre. Your heart rate is like 300 per minute." She was slowly regaining her composure, but still held onto my wrist, like it was a fragile link that kept us tied to each other.

I was quite accustomed to these visits, barging in uninvited for the past twenty-some years. It was my body's way of telling me I needed to slow down; otherwise, I would have kept going till I collapsed.

I'd been through numerous EKGs, echocardiograms, stress tests – you name it. I even wore a Holter monitor once. When one of the doctors suggested catheterizing, putting a tube into my thigh and pushing it all the way to my heart, I said I'd had enough.

I'd spent years researching the symptoms and causes, and found that it was likely sport-induced Supraventricular tachycardia. SVT. Sounded like an STD. At least for the latter, you got some pleasure out of acquiring it.

Eventually, my heart rate subsided to its normal rhythm. I asked Kate to give me a few more minutes to relax before we made our way back down. She gave me a kiss and said she'd explore the area for a bit and come back to get me.

I took a few deep breaths, reveling in the scenery and calming myself down. A couple of raindrops fell on my face from the dark cloud that was passing above – a welcome chill against my burning skin.

I rubbed my temples in the hopes of ridding myself of the headache lurking behind my eyes. The timing couldn't have been worse.

The ocean in front of me blurred, and everything around me disappeared into blackness. I leaned over and buried my face in my knees, slightly aware of the tingling sensation from the stone of the necklace as it touched my skin. When the pain in my temples dulled, I lifted my head, ready to embrace the next vision…

I was in the middle of a bedroom that looked eerily familiar. It was stylishly furnished, small, but comfortable. Two twin beds were pushed together to create one family bed (a common practice in Hungary owing to the lack of king sizes), which occupied most of the room. They were immaculately made up, not one wrinkle on the duvet cover.

Along the wall next to the bed (or beds) were two antique, intricately carved, deep mahogany dressers. Several shelves of books, neatly arranged, showing wear, decorated the wall above the beds. There was a glass door and two large windows that opened up to a balcony on the opposite wall. The windows stood open; the white curtains rose and fell in an intimate dance with the wind. Light penetrated the entire room, making it look much larger than it really was.

We were high up, perhaps on the topmost floor. The rooftops of many buildings were visible, spread across the city like a carefully designed labyrinth. I recognized Budapest. The city I was born in.

In the distance, the Liberty Statue – an oversized palm leaf held between her hands – towered over the city in mocking commemoration of Soviet Liberation by the "grateful" Hungarians. Even from afar, she looked mighty and proud on top of Gellert Hill, named after the unfortunate monk who, by bringing Christianity to the people, found himself thrown from its heights in a spiked barrel (Hungarians love erecting monuments to their suffering).

Muffled noises coming from another room pulled my attention away from the city. I took several hesitant steps toward a door that stood slightly ajar, lured by insatiable curiosity.

I stepped into a small, corridor-like kitchen. There was a table against the far wall, under a tiny window, through which bright sunlight seeped into the room, bathing the people sitting across each other in an angelic glow.

Liz was sipping on a glass of red wine, smiling and talking to a handsome man in a quiet, but animated manner. She was older, in her forties, perhaps; her short brown hair was streaked with gray.

The man was tall; even sitting down he was almost as tall as me. He was lanky, but muscular. His fine brown hair covered his forehead and enhanced his symmetrical features. He had a strong chin, but his smile softened the jawlines, making him look young. His striking features were captivating, so much so that it took me a moment to realize that he was not Balint.

He leaned forward to close the gap between them. A lovely vase filled with pale blue and white forget-me-nots sheltered their eager faces as he pulled her in for a kiss. They were holding hands and talking softly, as if worried that their voices would attract undesired attention.

I was about to turn around, feeling uncomfortable for trespassing on their intimate conversation, and somehow escape from this vision, when the man's expression suddenly changed. Confusion and pain distorted his handsome face. He clutched his chest in panic, knocking the vase off the table.

Fear permeated the air and shrouded the two lovers, their illusion of happiness shattering in that moment like the vase on the floor.

Shock and incomprehension paralyzed Liz as much as me. By the time she composed herself and crossed the table, the man lay on the ground, motionless, his eyes open, staring up into nothingness.

Liz was crying hysterically, cradling the man's head in her lap. Broken glass and trampled forget-me-nots lay scattered around them like a wreath…

Kate's hand on my shoulder jolted me out of my vision. The rain was coming down hard – unforgiving – washing away my tears.

"It's time to go," she said with a soft, but compelling tone.

I stood up, put my backpack on, and followed her down the rocks. I walked carefully, focusing on each step, preventing my mind from recalling what I'd just seen.

Chapter 15

1994
Budapest, Hungary

Summer camp. Pure hell. Seven weeks, twelve-hour days. Everything precedes with mandatory: practice, lunch, sleep, weights, practice. There is no escape.

We eat lunch at a restaurant across the street, a 10-minute walk from the club. It's still part of FTC, but built away from the main campus, sitting on the edge of a massive city-park that's mostly filled with people either sniffing glue or looking for trouble. I never come to this side, save for during the summer and even then, only to suffer through mandatory lunch.

I remember when food used to be sacred – fuel for the body. Now it's an abomination – the worst combination with puberty, as our curved assets are often attributed to eating too much, usually with off-hand sneering comments about having a few unnecessary kilos of love handle.

Overindulging is not an issue today, for I lose my desire to eat as soon as I see what's for lunch. Not a fan of meat, especially the ones that are coated in gooey fat. I fish out the most appealing piece, but I realize my mistake a bite too late.

I chew on it deliberately, but the fat sticks in my teeth, and the gelatinous, bitter taste makes me gag.

I grab the napkin and spit it out before I pull an Igor and ruin everybody's appetite. I wrap the chewy piece in the napkin, fold it in half, and tuck it neatly away, out of sight. I am faintly aware of a looming presence behind me, but I am too preoccupied by the lingering taste of lard to be bothered.

"What did you just spit out?" Dr. S.'s voice is too close for comfort.

I feel the heat of his body as he steps even closer. His breath encircles my neck in a chokehold, and his cigarette-infused coffee stench makes me gag again.

I pray to be able to keep the food down. I only spat out the chewy portion of the meat, so I don't think too much of the situation. However, by now, the entire restaurant has gone completely silent and gawking at us with blood-hungry eyes. I'm totally confused at his sudden irritation, and I feel my face burn with embarrassment.

I look at him with the most innocent expression I can muster. "Nothing," I say, but my guilt must be evident from my burning face.

He grabs the napkin and unfolds it, revealing the half-chewed goo of mess. He shakes his head; the color of permanent annoyance paints his pudgy cheeks, and finds its way to his vein-bulging neck.

It's disturbingly quiet; I don't want to look, but I am frighteningly aware of the unwarranted attention of the entire restaurant.

Dr. S. lectures me for a few minutes about my lack of honesty and the table etiquette my mother failed to indoctrinate me with and mocks the high standards with which I dare presume myself too good for this food.

He has the attention of the gaping crowd, swimmers and workers alike. He deposits the half-chewed slob back onto my plate with a provocative gesture, daring me to finish it off. Our gazes meet for a brief moment.

My mind races as I weigh my options: do I eat it and throw it back up, or continue to endure this humiliation? I can't decide. I'm dying inside.

I'm rescued by a sudden commotion outside that draws his attention away. With one last reproachful glare, he turns and walks away, leaving me to sulk in silence. The restaurant immediately returns to its usual noisy clamor – of chitchatting, of laughter, of clacking utensils – with a desensitized indifference.

After lunch, we (the seniors) take the commuter bus to the nearby elementary school. It's only two stops away, which is why it's one of Dr. S.'s favorite spots. Unfortunately, it hasn't been long enough to dull the painful memories accumulated over the many "precious" years I've had to endure here.

Entering the building tears up old wounds and leaves me bleeding inside. We find our designated room with our blow-up mattresses awaiting us. We deposited them the first day of camp and will collect them on the last day, which cannot come soon enough.

Dr. S. is a firm believer of napping; therefore, he instituted mandatory pre-afternoon-practice sleep. At first, it was difficult, but now I crave the sleep with every fiber of my being.

It doesn't take me long before exhaustion renders me comatose. The next thing I am aware of is Zoli's fidgeting on the rubber mattress, which sounds like nails on a chalkboard.

I reluctantly open my eyes, angry to be pulled away from sleep's delicious oblivion. The saliva stain on the headrest is a clear indication of my sweet slumber, which I already long for with burning desire. Ten more minutes before we have to wake, but in swimming standards, that's an eternity.

Seeing me awake, Zoli starts talking to me in a hushed voice, but I am too groggy to reply, which doesn't stop him from his incessant babbling. I lift my head to give him a death stare, only to catch Dr. S.'s accusatory eyes on me. There's no doubt he identifies me as the culprit of waking him. His berating look penetrates my soul and leaves me gasping for air. I put my head down, ready to cry out of frustration.

I gather my belongings, but before I can exit the classroom, Dr. S. stops me. Thankfully, he waits till everyone leaves. His look of disappointment feels like a gut-punch – I desperately wish he looked angry instead.

"I've had it with you," is all he says. He spits the words out like I spat out the rotten meat.

* * *

2012
Hagatna, Guam, USA

We took the next day off and decided to lounge around the hotel. Kate woke up early to beat the heat and took off for a run. I found refuge on the balcony listening to the soft hum of the sea spilling her waves on the sand, only to pull back teasingly like a coy lover.

I did not want to remember, to revisit my last vision, which was so out of sequence that it wasn't even part of the diary. Nagyi's life seemed like a series of catastrophes and every time I discovered a new chapter, it ended with heart-ache. And yet, the woman I knew was strong, self-assured, full of drive and love. How she found solace in all that bitterness eluded me.

In the end, the desire to know proved stronger than the promise of blissful ignorance. I opened the diary and found the entry where I'd left off. I caressed the letters with my fingers, tracing the soft curves as they stretched and looped around, here touching, here keeping a shy distance from each other, conversing in the intimate language of creation. The entry was dated May 1949.

I closed my eyes, and let my fingers feel the slight grooves of the paper, envisioning Nagyi's laboring hand carving her memories onto paper, letter-by-letter, word-by-word, giving them permanence.

I took slow, deep breaths, listening to the soft murmurs of the sea and the quiet sighs of the slowly waking city, my fingers resting on the page, willing myself to see her words come to life. I opened my eyes and watched the Philippine Sea disappear into darkness and Liz's silhouette come into view…

She stood in the kitchen, kneading dough with effort and precision. Her hair was in a bun, revealing her long neck, which was turning slightly pink from exertion. Though her hands moved like she was performing a well-rehearsed task, her movements were slightly awkward from behind.

The smell of fresh coffee and floury dough permeated the air, making my stomach growl with yearning for a little taste of home.

Liz's mom was sitting at the table, nursing her coffee, and attentively listening to the radio that lay on the kitchen table in front of her. Her long black hair was undone, covering her delicate shoulders, all the way to the middle of her back. Her face was smooth, not yet troubled by the chores of the day. Her dark walnut-shaped eyes were intently fixed on her coffee, her thick eyebrows drawn in deep thought.

I barely remembered my great-grandmother, Zsuzsanna – only that as a wee babe, I followed her around like an imprinted chick. Growing up, I was told that I inherited her wild spirit, her strong will, and soul-penetrating stare.

Both of them were preoccupied with their routine, but through their gestures and occasional smiles, their contentment draped around them like a warm, comfortable blanket.

Liz stopped kneading, patted the dough down with a couple of final taps to smooth it out, and cut three small slits on the top to let the bread breathe. She turned around, slightly balancing the cooking sheet on her huge, protruding belly. She must have been at least eight months pregnant. She placed the bread in the oven and leaned on the kitchen counter, caressing her belly with a happy smile.

There was a knock on the door. The two women were roused from their reverie by this untimely intrusion. Liz looked at her mother questioningly, who shrugged her shoulders in return.

"I'll get it," said Liz and walked out of the kitchen with a slight wobble.

In the door stood a skeleton of a man. He was tall (his head nearly brushed the top of the doorframe), but his thinness made him seem old and frail. He was filthy. His clothes were too big and drooped on him like clothes on a broken hanger. His face was hidden behind a thick beard, and his hair was matted with grime. His unwashed odor began to mask the aromas of breakfast. Hunger carved hollow grooves in his cheeks, visible even through the massive facial hair. A deep melancholy stared out from his small black eyes, the kind that makes you want to cringe and look away. The look of him made me want to cry.

The man's gaze landed on Liz's abdomen, his eyes growing large with disbelief. She withdrew a step in reaction to his scrutinizing look, holding her stomach in a protective embrace.

The sound of breaking china shattered the uncomfortable silence and drew their attention to the kitchen door, where Liz's mother stood pale-faced, grasping the doorframe for support. She cried out once with a sudden, wild abandonment that reached deep into her soul. The broken coffee cup lay at her feet, its contents staining the hardwood floor, seeping into the cracks.

The man's face relaxed; his eyes grew soft. He attempted a smile, but it disfigured his face, as if it were unaccustomed to the gesture. Liz looked back and forth between them before recognition suddenly dawned upon her.

"Father?" she asked, her voice rendered meek by disbelief and doubt...

Once more the Philippine Sea stretched out before me, singing her soft lullaby with each crashing wave. My fingers still rested on the paper, absentmindedly stroking the delicate curves of Nagyi's letters, which were illuminated by the sunrise glow of the necklace as it rested on the page.

June 1949

Father came home. After all these years, he finally found his way back to us. I didn't even recognize him when he showed up at the door. His appearance frightened me, looking all skin and bones, covered with grime, in desperate need of a bath. I'm still embarrassed by how sickened I felt at his appearance.

We didn't see much of him for the first week or so. He stayed inside his room, sleeping mostly. He slowly started coming out in the mornings, taking his coffee with Mother at the kitchen table. He sat there quietly for hours listening to the radio, lost in thought. He started to look more like himself, washed and shaven, but still terribly thin.

I had so many questions. Mother told me he was captured by the Soviets and was taken to Sevastopol, Crimea, where he'd spent the last four years in a prison camp. She didn't say more and made me promise not to press Father for answers, for he'd suffered enough. He is a changed man; the father who'd left us never returned home.

We're in Debrecen... came for a visit with my aunt, but we had to extend our stay because I went into labor. We named her Elizabeth. Balint insisted we name our children after us.

Holding Elizabeth in his arms, I watched Father smile for the first time since his return. Though I don't think he approved of us getting married without his consent, he immediately welcomed Elizabeth into his heart.

Father says we won't be returning to the city. Rather, we'll be moving to Felsogod, permanently... just as soon as I can leave the hospital.

Chapter 16

1995
Budapest, Hungary

I've accepted the fact that I am merely a disposable gear in a prodigy-producing machine where you either output excellence or get replaced. And since I'm neither outputting the desired excellence, nor leaving the club of my own volition, I am caught in the limbo of the *now what?*

I am a veteran. Only the pool rivals the longevity of my career, and even that has undergone renovations. Dr. S. still calls me "old fox" for safekeeping, but he no longer gives me the attention he once did: neither the good, nor the bad. I've learned to love and hate him. I live with the aching desire of wanting his approval, knowing that I'll never be good enough.

I envy those whose names, every four years, are hailed through the streets, satiating the country's hunger for worldwide recognition and national pride. I'm beginning to embrace my shortcomings as an athlete. Every day I train till my muscles ache, till my lungs burn, till my migraines become so unbearable that I can barely walk home.

I have become a slave to this grueling, mundane lifestyle.

* * *

2012
Tarzan Falls, Guam, USA

I let Kate talk me into yet another ingenious adventure: this time, to Tarzan Falls. She promised with unwavering confidence that it was a little over a mile, and even if we decided to veer off course – boonie-stomping, which I had no doubt was her intention – it would still only take us three hours, tops. I was reluctant at first, but when she swore up and down that the terrain would be easy, I caved.

After half an hour of driving mostly uphill, hugging twists and turns, we found the rest area off of Route 17 that served as the designated entrance for Tarzan Falls. Like most trail signs on Guam, this one was also invisible from the road. Perhaps the real giveaway was the vast collection of shoes dangling from the nearby power line.

"Are we here to buy some drugs?" I asked her, pointing at the colorful display of sneakers as we pulled in to park.

"Come now; you don't believe in that, do you? An open advertisement of your drug shenanigans?" she asked condescendingly, and laughed. "Drug dealers are not that stupid."

I gave her a questioning look.

She laughed again. "Not *that* stupid, Ollie."

"Okay, okay. Point taken," I said defensively. "Then what's with the shoes?"

She shrugged her shoulders. "I've heard it's a tradition… last hike on Guam, or something like that."

I looked down at my sandals and put my feet up on the dashboard.

"That would be quite the hefty *feat*," I said, wiggling my toes at her. "While I am the *sole* owner, there are still no strings attached."

Kate rolled her eyes at me, exasperated. "That was so bad," she said, but laughed, nevertheless.

We got out of the car and searched for the trail. We found the sign littered with bullet holes. Apparently, trail signs are considered a favored form of target practice among the natives.

Kate, equipped with a map and a compass and utter confidence, declared that this was going to be a piece of cake. Her satisfied, self-assured grin left me with little doubt. The path leading from the 'parking lot' was dry, clay-like dirt.

"We are nearing the end of the dry season," Kate said, kicking the dirt in front of her, sending a puff of dust into the air. "This will be all mud, come June."

I was thankful for walking on a dirt road, for I was certain Kate would lead us river-thrashing in no time. After our previous escapade through the sword grass, I considered myself a pro, and relying on Kate's promise of the easy hike, I opted to wear the least amount of clothing possible.

We hiked under semi-covered foliage for a while, sipping on water, enjoying the sporadic shade. Once we left the trees, the red clay road zigzagged through the top of the hill, like veins carrying blood, leading us to her heart.

We came to a stop. From where we stood, the terrain gradually sloped down, revealing an intimate network of hills and valleys. It was a massive organism, vast, like a desert. But instead of sand, the dunes were covered with sword grass, rocks, trees, and oasis-like jungles that indicated a hidden river nearby.

The trail curved to the left, but of course, Kate veered off the path with determined strides. I shook my head dejectedly, but knew better than to protest.

"The Ylig River is that way," she said, pointing to the east. "It's the largest river in Guam. If we aim toward it, we will stumble upon the Tarzan River, which will get us to the falls."

River thrashing. I was so right. But I held my tongue. She must have seen my miserable expression, sizing up the landscape that lay ahead.

"Come now, the grass is not that tall here," she said and winked at me encouragingly.

"Fool me once, Kate. But fool me twice?"

"Oh, ye of little faith," she said and ventured into the rugged terrain of grass and rocks, carving her own path down the valley.

With only one minor calamity involving Kate stepping on a beehive and suffering several stings to my amusement, we arrived at a flowing river and its charming swim holes, which were separated by elevation and several semi-submerged boulders.

We waded into its chilly, but refreshing depths, and sought refuge on one of the boulders that peeked out of the water, creating a soothing mini-waterfall in its wake.

We spread out on the rock, letting the river's current lull us into contentment. Here, with a heavy heart, I told her about my vision of Nagyi losing her second husband.

"Why did I have to see that?" I asked, wiping off my tears.

Kate looked at me contemplatively. "Perhaps for you to see that loss is part of life."

"Did she ever tell you what happened to him?" she asked after a stretch of silence.

I shook my head. "That's not something she would have shared. But Mom had told me the story before, and after seeing that vision, I put the pieces together. His name was Geza. He died of a heart-attack… one year into their marriage."

"That's so tragic," Kate said with a shake of her head. "Did she love him? I mean, love him like she loved your grandfather?"

"I am sure of it. But I know she never stopped loving my grandfather, either. The loss of their child broke their marriage, but not their love for one another."

"How do you know?"

"Because Nagyi tried to reconcile with him after Geza died, but it was too late. He, too, had already remarried."

We sat on the rock for a while before Kate urged us to keep going. We began to wade through the river with monotonous precision, hiking and occasionally swimming where the water got deep enough, lost in our own thoughts. But when the sun peaked, taunting us with her relentless heat, I began to voice my concerns.

"Kate, not to be pushy, but we have been fording this river for at least two hours."

She grunted, but kept pressing on. I held my tongue for another hour, but when I started running out of steam and water, and the river no longer kept me cool from the raging sun, I'd had enough.

"Kate, for crying out loud. This is not the Tarzan River, is it?" I said, irritated.

She gave me a penetrating look that sent chills down my spine. Even when she was utterly wrong, she hated to admit defeat.

"This has to be it. And even if it's not the Tarzan River, all rivers eventually lead out of the jungle," she said, her tone agitated.

In spite of my misgivings, I decided it wasn't worth angering her further. I endured the heat, the marching, and her morose attitude for another hour or so. "Kate, I hate to point out the obvious, but not only is this *not* the Tarzan River, it's also definitely not leading us out of here."

"I know!" she said, nearly spitting the words out, and pressed on stubbornly.

"This river is twisting and turning deeper into the jungle," I whined, nearly yelling after her, trying to catch up. I was tired and annoyed. "We left the car six hours ago, Kate!"

"I *know*!" she yelled back, but before she could say anything else, her knees buckled. I caught up to her just in time to catch her; otherwise, she would have face-planted into the water.

Her spell was momentary; she came to herself in my arms right away. I led her out of the water and made her sit down under a tree to escape the blazing sun.

"You don't have to prove yourself to me," I told her as gently as I could. I sat down next to her, weary.

She grunted in return, dazed, still collecting herself.

"We are lost, aren't we?" I asked, making sure my voice stayed as neutral as possible to avoid making the situation worse.

"Well, define lost," she said with a sheepish smile. "It's an island, so how lost can we be?"

I looked around to take in our rather hopeless situation: we were in a valley, surrounded by jungle, nowhere close to the intended trail, without anyone knowing where we were, going in circles in the hundred degree heat and humidity.

"I am going to take that as a rhetorical question," I said, masking my frustration at her wiseass remark. I offered her the last drop of my water. "Drink this."

She accepted it gratefully. We had no more water and we ate our snacks hours ago, but mentioning it would have been a moot point.

"We are done with this river," I said with a tone that left no room for argument.

"We'll rest here for a bit, until the sun is no longer directly above us, and make our way out that way." I pointed up the hill.

"You mean that way," she said, pointing the opposite direction with a self-assured smile.

I knew she had me; I was terrible with directions. I punched her shoulder lightly, feigning irritation. She lay down on the ground, laughing – an exhausted laugh that shook her entire body. I joined her, reveling in what little shade the trees along the banks provided.

The vertigo and nausea hit me as soon as I closed my eyes; my head spun as if I'd just lain down after too many glasses of wine. It felt like the ground was about to open up beneath me and devour me in one bite.

I sat up to avoid the urge to throw up – Nagyi's necklace dangled aimlessly on my wrist, drawing me into a near-hypnotic trance. When the dizziness subsided, I knew something was off…

The river in front of me was vast: nearly a mile-wide, murky, almost impenetrable swath of blue that flowed with a vengeance. It smelled of damp mud, fish, and residual boat oil. The air smelled different, too, like right before a spring rain. Massive, blooming poplar trees lined the shore, and the wind carried their cottonseeds that resembled fluffy snowflakes. I was in Felsogod.

A vivacious girl, no more than twelve, was throwing rocks into the river. The current carried her laughter, along with many fallen tree branches. Seeing my mother again in her youth was a rather uncanny feeling. She had my build, but life had gifted her with fuller proportions, visible even at her young age. Her eyes were like Peter's, though: small, beady, and almost accusatory as she kept looking back and talking incessantly at her mother.

Liz listened to her with motherly apprehension, as if anticipating inevitable mischief. She was in her thirties. Her brown hair came down to her shoulders in waves and danced coyly in the wind.

She looked unwell; her skin had a yellow hue to it, like an aging newspaper, and she was taking rapid, shallow breaths. My mother noticed it, too; she approached her, concerned.

Liz stood up, shaken and off-balance, and said she'd walk home. She bid her daughter to stay with her father, pointing toward a nearby bistro.

Knowing my mother, I wasn't surprised that she covertly followed Liz, worried for her well-being. It became a three-generation affair: each of us in pursuit of her own mother.

Liz stopped often, steadying herself on the fences that lined the street, only to collapse at her own gate. We both ran to her aid. I, once again, found myself in a state of impotence, tears of frustration obscuring my vision.

My mother remained levelheaded regardless of the blood that streaked down Liz's legs. She kicked open the gate and half carried, half dragged Liz down the long, narrow stone path to a covered veranda. Stepping inside, she carefully set her down on a solitary couch under an arched window. Liz was still unconscious and barely breathing at this point.

Before I could get my bearings, my mother was running out the door. I was paralyzed by indecision: should I stay or follow her? By the time I made up my mind, she was out of sight. Part of me knew nothing terrible could happen to my grandmother, since I'd spent my childhood with her, but it broke my heart to see her in such an exposed and fragile state. I wanted desperately to hold her hand, to kiss her, to do anything... anything, but stand there feeling useless.

Luckily, I was rescued from my internal agony by the rumbling noise of a small motorcycle as it sped through the open gate, down the narrow path, all the way to the doors of the veranda. An older man with a portly belly clambered off the bike, panting.

He had a black leather bag that opened on the top with a split-handle. A medical bag. I sighed with relief – a doctor. Elizabeth had run to fetch him. Smart kid. It was odd to feel pride at your own mother's resourcefulness, as if she were the child and I the adult.

The doctor began examining Liz thoroughly, muttering under his breath. My mother arrived, panting, and collapsed next to the couch. The doctor looked at her sharply. "I need to call an ambulance," he said with urgency.

She nodded, got up and led him inside the house. Liz's condition hadn't changed; her breath was still faint, almost non-existent. The doctor returned and monitored her vitals while young Elizabeth either hovered behind him or paced up and down in the small, enclosed area, biting her nails in agitation. The minutes passed with excruciating slowness.

"Why is it taking so long?" she asked him, uncharacteristically forthright as she spit a piece of her nail on the floor.

"It's coming from the city," he replied with surprising gentleness, overlooking Elizabeth's lack of decorum.

I presumed by 'city' he meant Budapest, roughly 15 miles away.

"Why?" she asked the same question that I was entertaining in my mind. It seemed foolish fetching an ambulance all the way from Budapest, when the nearest city was five minutes away.

"She must go to the capital… someone in her condition."

Noticing Elizabeth's frightened look, he patted her cheek gently. "You should go get your father," he said, and nudged her out the door.

Elizabeth looked at the doctor, alarmed. We both completely forgot about Balint. She spun around and took off running.

A wailing siren announced the arrival of the ambulance. Two burly paramedics staggered through the door, both sizing up the situation with detached dispositions. The doctor welcomed them with a firm handshake and immediately began talking to them with elaborate hand gestures. Their medical lingo was mostly incomprehensible, but I caught the seriousness of the situation by the multiple references to abdominal stiffness, bleeding out, and something like 'ektepic' pregnancy.

Liz was in the ambulance when Balint arrived with his daughter in tow. He was wheezing from the run, his eyes glinting with confusion and fear. He jumped into the back with the paramedics, instructing Elizabeth to stay put. The ambulance took off, trailed by its ominous siren.

Elizabeth stood beside the doctor, her face veiled with concern and the hurt of being left behind. The doctor put his arm around her in a comforting embrace. "You did right by coming to get me," he said with a soft, reassuring tone. "You just saved your mother's life."

Relief washed over my mother's face as she looked up at the doctor, tears in her eyes…

"Ollie? Ollie, are you okay?" I heard Kate's distant voice.

I sat hunched forward holding my head in my hands. I groaned loudly and began rubbing my aching temples.

"Another one?" she asked, gently caressing my back.

"Yup," I said, waiting for the headache to subside.

"We should get going," she said and stood up. "Can you make it?" She extended her hand and pulled me up. "I don't particularly want to spend the night here."

"That's not funny," I said, slightly panicked.

"I wasn't joking," she replied.

I suffered in silence as we began our ascent, bushwhacking our way out of the jungle through the trees and the ever-thickening maze of sword grass. I put an extra shirt in my bag (having already learned my lesson the hard way) and wrapped it around my right forearm for protection and to push the grass out of my way.

We reached a clearing, but it was only high enough to offer us a better view of the never-ceasing mounts of sword grass that stretched before us. I collapsed, dejected, bleeding from head to toe.

"I need a break," I whined, masking my inner wretchedness as best as I could. I looked at my watch – we'd left the car exactly eight hours ago.

Kate sat down next to me. "Five minutes," she said, "then we must continue."

"Yeah? Which way, Kate?" I asked, irritated.

"See that radio tower there?" She pointed to a tall, red and white tower peeking through the gap in-between two ridges.

"Mount Tenjo is the mountain behind it," she said, still pointing. "If we head that way, we'll get out."

"Today?" I asked, distrustful.

She laughed. "Yes, Ollie, within a couple of hours."

I shook my head, really hoping she was right. At this point I was starving, and all I could think about was French fries…

"Have you heard of 'ektepic' pregnancy?" I asked to divert my attention away from the growing pang of hunger.

"You mean, ectopic?" she said, correcting me as usual.

"Yes, that," I said, exasperated.

"It's an out-of-womb pregnancy. Why?"

"What does that mean?" I asked, confused.

"It's when the embryo doesn't make it to the uterus and attaches to the wrong place. Very dangerous. Can be life-threatening. Why?" She pressed again.

I shook my head. I didn't want to talk about it. Kate asked about the vision, but I ignored her question. Thankfully, she didn't press.

"I'm ready," I said, getting up.

We hiked aimlessly (or so I thought), battling our way through thickets and evil, vile sword grass. I was starving and dehydrated, growing lightheaded from the heat. In my daze, I thought I saw Liz appear and begin to walk beside me, following me with her ghostly visage.

"'It's silly to think you can sum up a person's life based on a few unrelated entries," said the apparition, teasing. "You won't find what you're looking for therein…"

"What?" I blurted out, staring at Liz, stupefied.

Kate stopped and turned around. "Did you say something?"

My gaze alternated between Liz, who stood there smiling at me knowingly, and Kate, who was waiting for me to reply. Clearly, Kate didn't see her. I shook my head vehemently. Obviously, I was hallucinating. We clambered on.

"You can't judge someone's life as if it were a series of random events, you know – life is not a photo album," Liz said, humming sweetly as she walked light-footed beside me.

Out of nowhere, another silhouette emerged. A tall, lean, handsome man with slightly boyish features took up walking next to me with long, heavy strides. His eyes were like a pouncing feline's, two slits of impenetrable blue.

"You quit our marriage," he said with an accusatory tone.

"Quit us, quit swimming, quit teaching… constantly dissatisfied, like you are too afraid to be happy… just like your mother. Running away from yourself doesn't leave you with much, now, does it?" he said, his voice full of spite.

I stopped and leaned on a tree to catch my breath and steady my trembling legs. Liz hovered there, looking at me with an expression that was half-concerned, half-daring. I reached out to touch her, but there was nothing there.

My ex laughed bitterly, shaking his head in disapproval as he slowly vanished out of sight. Guilt squeezed my heart, stealing my breath away.

"How could I have stayed in a marriage when I didn't even know myself?" I retorted defensively, finding my voice and courage at last, but he was nowhere in sight.

"You left… it was only supposed to be one year. You abandoned us…" said a familiar, disembodied voice through the tall grass.

"Dad?" I cried out, but received no reply.

I followed Kate, numb, my heart aching painfully with guilt. I didn't get far, before another shape appeared at my side. I felt a long-forgotten, but all-too-familiar fear stir within me.

"How foolish to think you'll amount to anything… anything at all," he said, shaking his balding head in disapproval.

His pudgy cheeks were flushed from irritation. His eyes were too small for his face, and yet they breached my defenses and left me exposed, vulnerable.

"Go away," I screamed and lashed out at him. Instead of Dr. S., my fist collided with a tree. His patronizing laughter echoed as he slowly disappeared.

Hearing my irate yelp, Kate stopped again. This time she walked back to me, her eyes wide with concern.

"Are you okay?" she asked tenderly.

"Just dandy," I said, sucking on my bleeding knuckles.

I pushed myself away from the tree and urged her to keep going. She obeyed reluctantly.

"Life is unpredictable," said Liz as she appeared once again at my side.

"Foolish to think you are in control," she said, her voice somewhat taunting. She was so close; I could almost feel her.

"Make plans, but be prepared for what life throws at you. It's all about the choices you make, Ollie… whether or not you react to life. How you face your tragedies defines you."

I stopped to face her, exhausted and beaten. The apparition vibrated slightly and it was now Nagyi who faced me, like the way I remembered her: short, mahogany-red hair, and deep-set wrinkles that complemented her mischievously tender eyes. She smiled at me with such warmth and love that my anger dissipated in an instant and left me completely overwhelmed. I broke down and cried.

"You've got to let go. Happiness is not a grand design, you know," she said in a quiet whisper as if consoling a child. "It's born out of tragedy, otherwise how would you measure it? Tragedy is unavoidable. Such is life. But happiness – *true* happiness – that's a conscious decision, and it's built on shared moments of fulfillment – of love." Her voice was gentle, her words achingly familiar.

She smiled at me one last time and reached out as if to touch my face before vanishing for the last time. I collapsed on the ground, surrounded by sword grass, and cried. Kate came back and sat down next to me, holding me in her arms until my tears dried up.

After ten long hours, aching and starving, head buzzing like an agitated beehive, we made it out of the thicket and found the main road. Kate took my hand and we walked in silence, feeling even more connected from this shared experience. We hitchhiked back to our car, miles away.

Chapter 17

1996
The Hill School, Pennsylvania, USA

There comes a time in your life when reality ceases to make sense and you begin to meditate on the idea of fate. Nagyi always says that coincidences are simply the instruments of fate.

I've just spent five weeks of my summer in the United States. Five amazing, precious, surreal, life-awakening weeks. I've learned rudimentary English and how to pantomime my basic needs in order to get by. I still can't believe that merely a month ago, all I knew about the US was through a TV show called *Dallas*.

I question the legitimacy of deserving this trip, but my cousin says that worthiness has nothing to do with it. "'Gifts are born from the pleasure of the giver, not from the merit of the receiver,'" she quoted one of her favorite books before I'd left. I don't really think she understands the magnitude of the role she's playing in changing my life, forever.

Dr. S. is upset that I took off before Nationals, (gossip travels fast in the club, almost as fast as gonorrhea), but even he couldn't prevent me seizing this opportunity.

I find refuge under a weeping Cherry Blossom tree, waiting for my taxi to take me to the airport; its faint pink foliage provides ample protection from the afternoon sun and soothes my sinking mood. I am the last one to leave, but I don't mind. I don't want to go.

I look around and catch a glimpse of a boy coming my way. He grins foolishly as he half walks, half trots toward me, twirling a ridiculous looking stick in his hand that he calls Lacrosse.

His name is Matt. He's talked to me every day during these past weeks. That is, he talks, I smile, he smiles, I attempt to talk, he shrugs, we smile. He is the sweetest thing – kind and genuine, even in his foreignness.

It's his eyes that pull me in, drowning me in their sadness. Eyes poisoned by a deep, unfulfilled desire for approval, the kind even his gentle smile can't hide. I recognize the look. I've lived with it all my life. It defines his solitary walk, even as he approaches me now, stick in hand. He doesn't seem to be surprised to see me, as if he's been expecting me to be here, waiting for him in this 300-acre empty campus, devoid of children, of laughter, of life.

He lives here. How lonely, to be surrounded by all this space and not a soul to share it with.

He sits down next to me. His wavy dark hair is combed neatly and parted fashionably to the side, like he is a special breed of this elite, preparatory school society. His slightly podgy, pre-pubescent cheeks are flushed. I can't tell if it's from his walk or if he's just self-conscious. He is wearing sandals of some kind, which I've learned is another staple of boyhood fashion around here.

He cracks open a can of Powerade and offers it to me. I shake my head and thank him. He continues to smile; it warms my heart.

We sit enveloped in silence. Words are unnecessary – our connection has taken root like this weeping tree we are sitting under and solidified into a powerful stem that will grow, bloom, wither, and revive with each season.

When the taxi arrives, he looks at me, his eyes damp with the tears of farewell. He hands me a haphazardly wrapped package and gives me a solid hug, another American custom.

As he holds me in his boyish embrace, I finally understand that the desire for acceptance, for approval, for validation is universal. It is a disease, a by-product of the human condition.

As the taxi pulls out, I watch him walk away, swinging his stick in the air. I taste a salty teardrop as it trickles into my mouth. I hold his departing gift in my lap, just as I hold onto the hope of seeing him again.

* * *

2012
Merizo Pier, Guam, USA

It was still dark outside, barely five-thirty in the morning when we left the hotel and headed to Merizo Pier at the southern end of the island.

Finding a place to park proved difficult, what with the popularity of the event and the lack of an actual parking lot. Cars lined up the side of the road for almost half a mile.

We left our belongings in the car and hid the key behind the fuel-tank door. We made our way to the check-in area, trudging through vegetation in our swimsuits, by the time the sun began to peek above the horizon, announcing her early-morning rise.

There were people everywhere, young and old, swimmers and non-swimmers alike, from all over the world gathering at the pier to test their skills and courage. Most of them were ready to go; giant black numbers decorated their arms and legs, clutching their bright swim caps (yellow for the amateurs and pink for the pros). They were lining up on the pier to take the ferry across to Cocos Island where the race to cross the two-mile lagoon began.

There was a soft, cool breeze coming off the ocean, a welcoming break from the stifling heat of midday. The early morning rays enhanced the coral gardens and sand flats of the lagoon, coloring the water diamond green.

People aboard the ferry were chatting excitedly, posing for pictures, or just sitting quietly, nervous for the event. It was a short trip to the other side. The ferry unloaded us, her first cargo, and turned around to fetch more brave souls.

The island was buzzing with the noise of newly arriving people and the endless chirping of caged native birds bred for the repopulation effort. We gawked at the exotic birds excitedly, but eventually the overwhelming stench of their guano dissuaded us from lingering there too long.

Volunteers lined the shore, offering water and Vaseline for the start of the race. Kate and I looked at the people suspiciously for spreading layers upon layers of goo on their bodies. Vaseline was common protection against colder waters.

"Isn't the water nearly 80 degrees here?" I asked one of them, curious.

"Oh, it's to protect against the jelly-fish," a stout guy answered nonchalantly as he dug his thick finger into the tube to spread another layer on his already goo-ed up arm. "It will prevent the stingers getting to your skin," he added, as he continued the dip - spread process.

Kate and I looked at each other skeptically, but we reached for the lube at the same time, nonetheless. Covered in Vaseline, we waded into the shallow waters, awaiting the horn that indicated the start of the race.

We lingered a couple of steps behind the pros, and some of the Olympians who traveled here for either the fame or the hefty prize, but a couple of steps ahead of the amateurs who posed more bodily harm due to their inexperience. The start of an open water race was often a bloody battle of kicks and punches until the herd eventually thinned out.

Once the horn went off, I fought my way through the melee. Without a clear sense of direction, the start was a chaotic tangle of limbs. To the nearby kayakers who were there to lead us to shore, we must have looked like angry sea creatures in the middle of a feeding frenzy.

Once I pulled away from the masses and positioned myself close to the front, the swim became a steady rhythm of stroke and breath. As long as I kept a swimmer to my left, I didn't need to bother navigating. I enjoyed the slight burn of exertion in my arms and lungs – a sensation I was both accustomed and addicted to.

I allowed my mind to settle into a meditative state of here and now. Swimming was an intimate dance with the water – a communion based on respect in a collaborative expression of love. We danced in synchrony, anticipating each other's move. One stroke at a time.

And after twenty some years, I thought of Dr. S., of the man who shaped my childhood, stirring up a mixture of resentment, anger, confusion, respect, and even love.

I pondered my choices as I swam through the warm, salty lagoon. I could choose to live a life of resentment and continue denying, as I have these past seven years, an essential part of me: swimming. Or I could choose to embrace my love for the sport and be thankful for the passion and drive Dr. S. instilled in me. And with each breath, each stroke, I continued to let go, because there was only one thing that mattered. I was born to swim.

I felt like a new person after the race, like I'd shed my old skin and replaced it with a new one.

"I decided to train again," I said, my voice full of the same passionate excitement that I'd felt re-ignited in my heart during the race. Kate looked at me, surprised.

"The World Masters Championships is in two years. In Montreal, Canada. I'm going to swim the 200 Fly and I am going to win it," I declared with zeal.

"That's my girl," she said, beaming with pride.

She didn't question how I knew the location and date of the Championships. I was surprised myself; perhaps this was long coming.

We made it back to the car. Kate retrieved the key, her face wreathed by a satisfied smile as she hopped behind the wheel. We sat in the car for a few minutes, still in awe of our two-mile swim.

"How about some pizza and a margarita for breakfast?" she asked and raised her eyebrows at me, temptingly. It was barely 10 in the morning.

"Sounds about right," I said and leaned my head back, smiling.

"Should we change, first?" I asked, as we still had our swimsuits on.

"Nah," she said, shaking her head. "Why bother? This is our last day on Guam. Let's go out with a bang," she said with a laugh, and playfully slapped my thigh.

She pulled the car out and made a U-turn, heading back toward our side of the island. "Where are you going to train?" she asked as she accelerated, bringing the conversation back to swimming.

"There has to be a few Masters teams around Boston. It shouldn't be too difficult to find one," I said, looking out the window, saying my silent good-bye to the retreating shoreline.

"And who are you going to represent?" she asked.

"What? At Worlds?" I asked, still glued to the window, preoccupied with my mournful farewell.

"Where else, you goof?"

I pulled myself away from the view and looked at her with a grin. "I'm going unattached."

Chapter 18

1996
Budapest, Hungary

I got home from the US just in time for Hungarian Nationals. Dr. S. avoids me like the plague… or that's what I tell myself. His avoidance is not deliberate, but rather born out of indifference.

I am confident, excited, and ready to prove myself in the 200 Butterfly, my favorite event ever since Lacika's unfaltering faith in my ability. I didn't miss a single workout while in the US, knowing the importance of this meet.

The official whistles. I step up on the block. I glance to my left where Eger… that is Krisztina Egerszegi (the youngest Olympic gold medalist ever!) stands, ready for the race. She looks intimidating, relaxed… majestic as she grips the block, her long, perfect fingernails shining with the reflection of the untouched pool.

A moment of doubt flashes through my mind. I chase it away with anger and steady my trembling legs, reminding myself that if Lacika believed in me, then so should I.

The gun goes off. I dive. All doubt and nervousness dissolve the instant I enter the water. Relax, I tell myself… it's a 200. Keep your head down. Breathe. Focus on your stroke.

Breathe. One up, one down. Breathe. Turn. Still in the lead! Breathe. Pick up the tempo. Breathe. Turn. Add in the legs. Breathe. Don't drop your hips. Breathe.

Last 50. My lungs burn, my legs ache, my arms feel like lead. I see people ahead of me. Close your eyes, I tell myself. Swim your own race. Bring it home. Breathe.

Each breath sears my throat as I undulate forward to take another stroke. Breathe. I shut out the pain: kick, kick, kick is all I think about. I've got to make Dr. S. proud. Into the wall… don't breathe.

I touch the electronic pad with a powerful stroke. It hurts. It hurts so good! I look up at the scoreboard. I take my fogged-up Swedes off to see it better. My heart is pumping like crazy. It can't be. I can't believe it. I did it. I keep looking at the time, stupefied. I medaled. I. Actually. Medaled.

I linger at the wall searching the stands for Dr. S. The official yells at me to exit the pool. I grab my FTC robe and walk back to the team, exhilarated. They greet me with cheers and hugs. I can't stop smiling. I look around. No sign of Dr. S.

"Where is he?" I ask Niki, still looking around. My body trembles slightly from the residual nerves and built-up lactic acid in my muscles.

"I don't know," she replies and shrugs her shoulders, surprised that I would ask. "He went downstairs a while ago," she adds, looking at the stairs.

Downstairs.

There is a billiard saloon, recently built underneath the swimming pool. It stretches the entire building and it has a full bar. Most swimmers find entertainment and release there after meets.

I catch Zoli coming upstairs from the direction of the double doors that lead to the saloon, talking to Mike, our friend from a different club.

"Have you seen Dr. S.?" I ask him, interrupting his conversation with Mike.

He frowns at me, slightly annoyed for cutting him off in mid-sentence, but doesn't hesitate to reply. "Sure," he says with a slight shrug. "He is having a drink at the bar."

I collapse on the bench, exhausted. It's difficult to swallow my disappointment. Niki sits down next to me and attempts an encouraging smile.

"It's okay," I say unconvincingly, and wipe the angry tears away. "I'm leaving, Niki."

She doesn't seem surprised. "I know," she says with a quivering voice. "I've known it for a while… I just hoped it wouldn't be this soon."

She takes my hand and squeezes it gently. "I'll miss you." Tears glint in her eyes, as well. "Promise me you'll write and tell me all about your life in this big ol' USA."

I force a smile. "I promise."

* * *

2012
Hagatna, Guam, USA

I went for a solitary walk to properly say good-bye to Guam, the island that has nurtured my spirit back to life. It was time to let go of my demons and to finally see myself for who I was – to love myself without conditions, without limitations, without needing anyone's approval. It has been a strange journey: one of letting go, of healing.

I walked along the beach, my feet cradled by the intermittent waves that tickled my toes with their soft caresses, erasing the footprints I'd just left behind. Footprints as ephemeral as life – washed away by time.

I thought of John, whose memory has faded with the years, but whose love had burrowed itself into my heart, like a sand crab that digs its claws into the sand to prevent itself from being dislodged and washed away by the relentless waves.

I can't recall the year he left us, only the weather, as if our memories were attached to markers of the season. Michigan had plenty of them: like the vibrant pinkness of the blossoming cherry trees, the unforgiving tornados that uprooted trees, the white blizzards that buried cars, or the thunderous calls of cicadas announcing summer's arrival.

It was a day like that. Winter's last remnants were still visible in the semi-lifeless trees, but spring's perfume already hung in the air, luring college students out from their hibernation. It was early in the morning; the air was chilled, but warm enough to tempt them outside, desperate as they were for Vitamin D.

It was exam week. My junior year in college was coming to an end. It was difficult not to notice the juxtaposition of a blooming spring and the wilting days of my college life. I was sitting on the steps of my ridiculously expensive, albeit dilapidated college house, under the pretense of studying.

My textbook remained untouched, vying for attention as I gazed mindlessly at the narrow side street that ran straight into our house, like a tiny periscope, offering a glimpse of the activities taking place on the busy main stretch.

Laura, one of my six roommates who shared the heavy burden of paying the exorbitant rent, settled next to me with a heavy sigh – a sigh only a college student facing the imminent hours of exam angst could make.

The wail of an ambulance siren out of nowhere cut our nonsensical chat short. We both instinctively gazed toward the main street, detached, yet drawn by morbid curiosity, feeling that fleeting twinge of pain only a wailing siren can bring. It was too beautiful of a morning for such an intrusion.

Yet, just beyond the corner, sheltered from our sight, John exhaled for the last time. He went for a jog that morning – must have been inspired by the spring's breath in the air, because he normally hated running. We sat two blocks away, oblivious of his pain, of the impending loss. John was a tremendous athlete, and yet, it was his heart that couldn't bear the weight of a jog…

The crashing of the waves snapped me out of my reverie. I found myself at a secluded spot on the beach, near the end of the bay where massive rocks prevented me from walking any further.

I faced the Philippine Sea, mesmerized by its immensity and power. I was but a tiny, insignificant spot in the vast universe, and yet the desire to live, to make a difference, burned in my heart like a once-dormant volcano, ready to wake and erupt.

Susan, the shrink, was right, I thought. The time for living in fantasy was over.

Like first love. My fantasy version was filled with romantic gestures, candles, and unparalleled bliss. I was 19 when I'd met John. I didn't believe in *love at first sight*, but when I'd walked into the room full of strangers and our eyes met, I knew our lives would collide. Reality: no candles and no magical gratification of a romanticized first night. I lost my virginity in the dingy, mold-ridden, beer-stinking basement of a college house, which became the staple of our relationship.

Foolish love? Definitely. Romantic? As much romance as college parties could provide. But it lasted two years with a full complement of break ups, bitter fights, rejections, and lame attempts at reconciliation. Teenage love. But death quickly quells the quarrels and leaves only the loving memories and that unfillable hole behind.

I wouldn't change my memories for any fantastical romance. Reality is no bastard child, I thought. Reality is what I make of my life.

I sat down on the shore, noticing for the first time that I was still clutching Nagyi's diary in my hand. It looked up at me solemnly, feeling unnaturally heavy in my grasp. I admired the orange stone of the necklace, dangling from my wrist, as it glinted enticingly in the sunshine, slightly grazing the faded cover. I had told Kate again and again that it must have magical powers, granting me visions of Nagyi's life.

"Nonsense," she said, when I'd brought it up again after our ten-hour-long *mis*adventure. She'd grabbed my wrist and closely examined the stone like she did the last time I'd shoved my hand in her face.

"The stone is not magical," she'd declared then with conviction, pulling me in by my hand to plant a kiss on my cheek. "It's your love, Ollie. Your connection with your grandmother – that's what's magical."

I'd been putting off thinking about the day Nagyi had passed for nearly two years. I knew it was time to let go. I closed my eyes and willed the memory to come to life…

I sit on my mother's bed, watching Nagyi sleep; so frail, she is nearly swallowed up in the sheets. Mother brought her home from the hospital so that she can die peacefully, surrounded by comfort and love.

Once a fierce woman, she looks shrunken and fragile: her short hair is disheveled, her skin is pale, and her cheekbones are sunken in. I carefully brush the stray strands away from her forehead, afraid that my touch will somehow cause her pain. I desperately wish I had more time with her.

I get lost staring at her hand; it's so small in my grasp. That hand has guided me so many times… taught me how to count using my fingers, how to play cards, how to solve crossword puzzles, how to eat sunflower seeds properly. She took me to swim practices when my parents were at work, tucked me in at night, baked delicious desserts, canned the most magical apricot jams, wiped off the tears I'd shed in my childish fits. When I asked her questions, she always answered without sugarcoated exaggerations, without sheltering me from the truth.

Love grips my heart with overwhelming strength. I wish I had the power to wrest her from her disease, her pain, from the clutches of death.

Our bond reaches deeper than family, yet growing up, I knew nothing about her beyond the fact that she was my grandmother and that I loved her. She was always so preoccupied helping, supporting, and worrying about others that she forgot to live for herself.

She is still sharp as a tack when awake, smiling at me, easing my pain at her impending loss. It is her failing liver that pulls her into fits of incoherent stupor, lasting longer each time. She was suffering from gallstone and she insisted on surgery despite our protest, despite the warning that her liver was stressed enough with Hepatitis C. She was stubborn. She is stubborn.

"Olive," Nagyi says, pulling my attention to her face. Her eyes are open, looking at me with so much love that my throat constricts.

She is full of concern, as if our roles are reversed. "You are troubled." Her voice is cracked. "Your heart is heavy with doubt and pain."

Of course I am troubled. She is leaving me. I watch a teardrop make its way down her cheek. I wipe it off and give her a reassuring smile. "I am fine," I lie.

"Nonsense," she retorts grudgingly. "You carry your troubles in your eyes, just like your mother," she catches me in my lie, like she always does. I can feel my mother's anguish behind me, without looking.

"It's time to let go of your demons," she continues. "Don't wait until it's too late to realize you have not yet lived. The past should not have such a strong hold on you. If you let your past consume you, the present will slip through your fingers. Without the present, there is no future to build. The past will become your life." Her voice is urgent, full of warning.

"Look at me," she squeezes my hand, but her grip is weak. "Life is precious and time is fleeting. Amidst all, regret is like a bully; the more you let him taunt you, the stronger hold he will have on you. Don't let the demons of the past jeopardize your happiness," she says with a deep, resonant, yet caring voice. "Remember, happiness is a choice."

"I promise," I say as I kiss her hand.

She smiles in return and closes her eyes. Her wrinkles vanish; she looks graceful and at peace. My mother, exhausted by sadness, pulls her chair closer to me. I admire the strength of her composure. We say our wordless goodbyes, and I find the land of tears…

I opened my eyes.

The wind picked up slightly, caressing my skin with her cool, soft touch and drying up my tears. I shed my clothes and waded into the water to cleanse myself of the sadness and the loss, gripping the diary in my hand.

Liz's voice echoed in my head. '*It's silly to think you can sum up a person's life based on a few unrelated entries… You can't judge someone's life as if it were a series of random events, you know – life is not a photo album.*'

How foolish was I to think I needed words to remember her by? I was part of her. She was part of me. It was time to let go of the pain of her loss, of the guilt I felt for leaving my home, for feeling that I was never good enough, for constantly seeking validation. The past had no hold on me. Life was precious and I had only one to live.

I opened the diary and pushed it under the water, watching the ink dissolve and fade away into nothingness, no longer bound to this world.

To the friends and woes, and the sleepless nights;
To the courageous failures in the forest of life;
To the laughter and tears, beyond the bounds of pain;
To the demons of the past, shaking their angry chains.
To the restless souls in the crowd of darkness,
Daring to light a path with their sun-sodden steps of defiance.